SEALED WITH A TRYST

ORDINARY MAGIC - BOOK 7

DEVON MONK

ODD
HOUSE
PRESS

Sealed With a Tryst

Copyright © 2022 by Devon Monk

ISBN: 9781939853257

Publisher: Odd House Press

Cover Art: Lou Harper

Interior Design: Odd House Press

Print Design: Odd House Press

SEALED WITH A TRYST

Delaney Reed needs a vacation from her vacation town. Even on a good day, it's a lot of work to keep the peace in a town full of gods, monsters, and magical beings. Lately all the good days have gone from bad to worse. Luckily, Delaney has a plan to steal away with her fiancé, Ryder Bailey, for a nice relaxing weekend together.

Her getaway plans come to a screeching halt when Delaney discovers Crow's garage sale is selling cursed magical items to anyone who wants one—and everyone wants one.

Delaney only has a few hours to hunt down the cursed objects before a massive winter storm barrels into town and her vacation escape becomes impossible. But Delaney isn't going down that easily. Neither rain, curse, nor killer sea monster or love-sick Bigfoot will keep her from getting three blissful days alone with the man she loves—hopefully far, far away from Ordinary, Oregon.

For my family,
and all the Ordinary dreamers

CHAPTER ONE

I PARKED the Jeep and stared through the rain at my almost-uncle, Crow, who was actually the trickster god Raven. He was waiting just inside the mouth of the tent he'd set up in front of his glassblowing studio. As if he'd been expecting us.

"Ten bucks it's all stolen." My youngest sister, Jean, wore a beanie over her blue hair, the bangs across her forehead making her eyes sky bright. She had on a puffy jacket with her badge on it, just like me. Although my badge said Chief Reed and hers just said Officer Reed.

Crow wiggled his fingers at both of us. His smile was white against his russet-tan skin, and his dark hair hung past his shoulders. He'd braided that hair and added a feather earring to his outfit today. Crow feather, of course.

"I mean, sure," I said. "At least some of that stuff must be hot. This is Crow we're talking about. But what I can't figure out is the whale."

We both leaned forward to better see out the windshield.

The January wind buffeted the Jeep hard, rocking it on its springs. Rain hammered down on the metal roof like rocks thrown from the heavens. A storm front was pushing in off the Pacific. Torrential rain would hit by tonight. Then we'd see winds clocking in at sixty miles an hour and gusting to eighty.

Just another wet, windy, possibly deadly January day in Ordinary, Oregon.

"The whale I understand," Jean said, as we stared at the tent. "It's a tent, we're a beach town. Matchy-match. But why is it that… color?"

"Lurid pink?" I suggested.

She nodded. "Don't get me wrong, I love me some color, but there's something about that thing that makes me want to stab it."

The hot pink whale flapped its obscenely large mouth, flailed its flippers, and flipped its tail like it'd just heard Jean's threat and was trying to swim away.

But no matter what Jean or I thought about the thing, there were people moving around inside that ridiculous tent. Shoppers couldn't resist a bargain, even in this weather.

Crow, still watching us, pointed upward with both hands.

The whale's head was topped with a blow hole, and out of that sprayed blood red streamers. An additional banner near the startled whale eye declared: whale of a sale

"Is this an exploding whale thing?" Jean asked.

"Because we weren't the town that blew up that rotting whale in the seventies."

"I think this is a Crow thing. Which means it's nothing but trouble. Let's see what he conveniently 'found lying around' to sell." I flipped up my hood and pulled it tight under my chin.

"Think we'll need cuffs?" Jean asked.

"Only if he won't show us where he stashed the stolen traffic light."

We both pushed out of the Jeep, muscling against the wind.

Ordinary was a little beach town created by gods who wanted to put their powers down and vacation as humans. The Reeds had been chosen ages ago to be the guardians of the town, to uphold the laws, both supernatural and human.

Being the eldest Reed sister meant I was not only the police chief, I was also the Bridge—the one who let gods into the town and helped them put their power to rest. I also kicked them out when necessary and kept all the supernaturals and humans who lived here safe.

It was hard work, sometimes 24/7 work. Even though I loved it, I'd found myself a little more worn out lately. Things had not been calm the last few years.

"Delaney!" Crow called out over the wind and rattle of rain on the tent. "Jean. What brings you two out here today?"

"Where's the traffic light?" I ducked into the mouth of the whale and quickly scanned the tables and shelves that filled its belly.

It looked like a regular rummage sale: kitchen items,

small furnishings, little piles of tools, and folded clothing. Other things like jewelry boxes, vases, and carvings were scattered throughout. Pretty little red and gold cardboard boxes had been tucked in the corners and out-of-the-way spots.

"Traffic light," Crow mused. "Hmmm. I'm gonna say... above the intersection."

"We know you took it," Jean said. "Hey, are those brownies?"

"Help yourself. There's coffee, too."

She threw me a look, and I nodded.

It was wet and cold and had been wet and cold for months. Coffee was the only way to get through Oregon's never-ending season of gloom, otherwise known as October to June. July couldn't get here fast enough.

"I thought you weren't going to do a sidewalk sale in January. In the middle of a storm," I said.

"And I thought you were going on vacation." He looked me over from head to foot, his clever eyes missing nothing. "Boo Boo. Are you okay? Are you and Ryder fighting? You got the pre-wedding blues? Talk to Uncle Crow."

Nope. No way. Not going to discuss my love life with a trickster god.

"How about Uncle Crow tells me what he did with the traffic light?"

The corner of his mouth rose, and his eyes curved into crescents. "Why do you think I did anything with it?"

I waved a finger at the impromptu garage sale we

were standing in the middle of. "You have a thing for selling off bits of Ordinary any chance you get."

He made a sound and slapped his hand over his heart. "Wounded. You know I do just fine with the glass shop. This is only to drive traffic to my Blow Your Own Balls class."

"Really wish you'd rename that thing."

"No, you don't." He waggled his eyebrows, and he was so much my uncle in that moment, so much the man I'd known since I was a kid, that it was everything I could do not to laugh.

"Nice record collection." Jean strolled over, balancing two Styrofoam cups and a brownie wrapped in a napkin. "Anything valuable?"

"Couple of them," Crow said, much to the interest of the gray-haired woman who was following Jean back from the snack station and obviously eavesdropping. "If someone had a good eBay shop, they could turn a tidy profit."

The woman stilled, then hurried back to retrieve her companion, a woman who could have been her sister.

"You sly dog, you," Jean said, as she handed me one of the coffees. "Look at you driving up sales. Now I know why you put up a whale tent."

"Oh?" Crow asked, all innocence.

Jean nodded. "They're buying this stuff hook, line, and sinker."

"Delaney," Crow said, "your sister is making me look bad in front of customers."

"By telling the truth?" I said sweetly. "Also, we're not customers."

Crow scoffed, but I was paying more attention to the ladies who had pounced on the boxes of records and started flipping.

"Jim Croce!" the eavesdropper shouted to the other.

"What?"

"Bad Bad Leroy Brown!"

"I have cream for that!"

"Time in a Bottle!"

"Oh, no, dear. You don't want to put it down there!"

"Croce! Croce!"

"Well, what I do with my crotchy is none of your business."

"No. The songs! Jim Croce!" She waved the album at her friend who gasped.

"The record player!" Two gray heads swiveled, their eyes glittering with Black Friday glee.

Crow cleared his throat to get their attention and pointed toward the tail of the tent.

"Get it!" one shouted.

"Over there, over there!" the other said.

They were off in a flash, zeroing in on an old suit-case-style record player that sat on a pile of crab traps and rusted Christmas tree stands.

For a second, just a flash, I thought the record player glowed with yellow light, but then the wind whipped, buckling the whale's tail, and the yellow light—if it had even been there—was gone.

"So, seriously. Where did you get all this?" I asked.

"Is that an accusation I hear in your voice? It sounds like you're trying to accuse me of something."

"I can throw you in jail for annoying me, you know."

"Like you would."

There was that. I didn't abuse my station here. None of us on the force did. Upholding Ordinary's laws meant none of us were above those laws. We followed the rules—all of them, both supernatural and human.

"Theft is still a crime," I said. "So… maybe you want to just tell the truth here."

"Storage units."

I took a drink of the coffee. It was good. Rich. "Whose storage?"

"No one's." At my look, he shook his head. "Abandoned. People move out of this town, you know. They stop paying storage bills then their units go up for sale. I'm surprised you didn't know that's how it worked. They made a whole TV show about it once."

Jean snorted, even though her mouth was stuffed with brownie. "Fake TV show," she mumbled.

"Totally staged," he agreed. "But all this?" He raised his hands like a king displaying his land. "All of it purchased by me—legally," he added. "Wanna look around? Maybe you'll find something to remove that stick out of your—"

"—asshole!" A teen laughed.

Crow's eyebrows rose, and he pointed over his shoulder at the kid, Keith, a werewolf.

He and the shapeshifter, Fernando, were around the same age. Fernando held a big, old hourglass up and away from the werewolf's reach.

"I saw it first," Fernando said, "But for the low, low price of three hundred dollars, I might be willing to part with it."

Keith crossed his arms and scowled but could only hold it for a second before he smiled. "The sticker says ten bucks, doofus." He shoved his friend.

Fernando lowered the hourglass. Once again, I thought I saw a glitter of gold, but it was gone so quickly, I was left blinking my eyes and wondering if it was just eyestrain.

"Toss me five," Fernando said. "We can use it for game night."

"Deal." Keith dug in his back pocket for his wallet, and the two boys moved on to the next table, laughing about a collection of busted plastic lightsabers.

"All right," I said. "So all this is legally yours."

"That's what I've been saying all this time. Glad you finally caught up."

Jean had finished the brownie. She wadded the napkin and stuck it in her coat pocket. "What about the traffic light?"

"Is this a trick question?"

"Did you steal it?" I asked.

He threw his hands up. "Why would I want a traffic light? They're kind of hard to sell and heavy as hell, which means no one would want to pay shipping for it."

That was true. "Then you won't mind us looking around for a few minutes?" I asked.

"Knock yourself out. Buy something pretty for your boyfriend."

"Fiancé," I corrected.

"When's that wedding, again?"

"We haven't set a date."

"Too bad you don't have time for a little vacation.

Sounds like a planning session is in order. But don't let me give you any wild ideas." He winked, then headed over to the counter where he had an old-fashioned cash register and a very modern card reader set up to handle the purchases. The two record ladies were already in line, and the hourglass boys were right behind them.

Jean and I stood there a minute studying the crowd and the piles of junk.

"So," she said.

"No."

"You don't even know what I'm going to say."

"I can guess."

"It could be anything."

"All right," I said. "Surprise me."

"You were supposed to go on vacation today. You and Ryder. What happened?"

I glanced at the vampire in the corner who was studying a gold pocket watch through the jewelry loupe at his eye.

"He's been leaving brochures everywhere," I said.

"Ryder?"

I nodded and walked the perimeter of the place. "Tropical beaches, mountain cabins, cities, canyons."

"You got in a fight over vacation brochures?"

"No."

She picked up an old eggbeater. Waited.

"It's just that he's been planting them everywhere!"

"Here we go," she muttered, turning the crank and making the beaters spin.

"I keep telling him yes, but stuff keeps coming up.

So we've had to cancel. A lot. The fees are starting to add up."

"Uh-huh."

"It's not like I don't want to get out of town."

"Of course not."

She spun the beaters in the air, and the wind outside heaved the whale sides, sucking the tenting in, and blowing it way out. Rain clattered again, driving hard.

"I have a lot on my plate," I said, but even as the words were out of my mouth, I knew they were a lie. Or at least an avoidance.

I *did* want to leave town. Desperately. The idea of a vacation with my fiancé was… well, it was wonderful.

But a little part of me, just a tiny slice of my heart, was frozen, stuck here, worried what would happen to the town if I were gone.

When our father had died, just a few years ago, I'd stepped into his place as the Bridge and Chief of Police all in one go. A lot had happened since then. I'd been shot, lost my soul, regained it, been attacked by demons, killed by an ancient evil.

I'd fallen in love with the boy I'd adored growing up. The boy I'd had a crush on. The man who'd returned to his childhood town.

Ryder Bailey.

It was easy to want to go away with him.

It was impossible to find a break in the constant troubles in this town. Every time I thought I could grab a full twenty-four hours, or maybe stretch it to a three-day weekend, something blew up.

Literally.

"You know," Jean said, "a new horizon would be really good for you. You've been through a lot in the last… well, years."

"It hasn't been—"

"—and so has Ryder." She tossed the eggbeater back on a pile of kitchen utensils and small animal statues, then caught my gaze. "Both of you need time together."

"We have lots of time together. We live together."

"Time alone. Out of town. Away from your jobs." She planted her hands on her hips and that Reed stubbornness set her stance.

"I see you have no opinion about this."

She opened her mouth, probably to lecture me on my relationship, but my phone rang. I pulled it out and turned half away from her to answer it.

"Chief Reed."

"Delaney," said Frigg, who was the Norse goddess of the same name. "Aren't you out of town yet?"

"You know I'm not." I was pretty sure the gods and goddesses would know when I left. They'd feel the Bridge closing.

"Since you're still here, I need to talk to you."

"I'm listening."

Jean *tsk*ed and shook her head. I scowled at her and pointed at the Chief part of Chief Reed on my coat.

"In person," Frigg said. "How about the Blue Owl?"

I glanced around at Crow's stuff, then at the scattering of new people coming in the tent mouth, shaking off the rain, and browsing through the treasures.

I could have sworn another flash of gold twinkled at

the corner of my eye, but when I turned that way, all I saw was normal, everyday junk.

No gold sparkles on any of it.

My phone vibrated.

"Delaney?" Frigg asked.

"Hold on."

I pulled my phone away from my ear so I could scan the screen. Text message from Ryder with an attachment.

I tapped the message.

All it said was: *yes?* above a photo of a gorgeous high mountain lake with a sweet cottage sitting like a storybook jewel above the curve of the shore.

My heartbeat sped up and I froze for a second. It looked idyllic. But we did not need one more cancellation fee. I hoped he hadn't booked it yet.

I closed the text and held my phone back up. "I could eat," I told the goddess. I cleared my throat. "See you there in about twenty?"

She chuckled. "I don't know what's going on with you, but I look forward to hearing about it. Oh, and bring the dragon. I have something for it."

I hung up and spotted Jean. She'd wandered off during the call and was now standing in the checkout line.

"Jean?" I called.

"House hippo!" She held up a little statue and gave it a wiggle.

"Why?"

"Because it's a house hippo." She almost had to

shout over the rain. Crow, dishing out her change, glanced over at me and wiggled his eyebrows.

"They're good luck," he said, while Jean made big eyes and nodded vigorously.

I sighed and made a wrap it up signal.

She took the hippo and a paper-wrapped something Crow handed her, then strode over. "Something go down?" she asked, as she fell into step with me.

"Frigg needs to talk over lunch."

"Thank gods," Jean said. "I'm starving. Here." She offered me the paper-wrapped package. "It's a cookie. You look grumpy."

I thought about opening it, but we were at the lurid pink mouth of the lurid pink whale, and beyond that was a downpour so heavy, the rain was a wall of white.

Staying inside the whale was suddenly sounding like a better idea.

"So I heard about this great hotel up on the Olympic Peninsula," Jean started. "They have this vacation deal…"

And just like that, I was out in the rain and running for the Jeep, my sister laughing and splashing right behind me.

CHAPTER TWO

THE BLUE OWL was Ordinary's only twenty-four-hour diner, and it was a favorite of truckers hauling up and down Highway 101. Even with a detour to pick up the dragon pig, we got there in under ten minutes.

The smell of onions and butter and fresh bread hit me as I clomped through the door, dragon pig tucked under my arm. Over the scratchy old speakers, the Big Bopper sang about big-eyed girls and Chantilly lace.

Outside, the stormy day grew darker even though it wasn't even evening yet. The storm was gonna be a beast of a thing. I hung my coat on the rack by the door, scanned the room, and headed over to the booth by the window to meet with a goddess.

Frigg saw Jean and me coming, smiled, and waved at the table already loaded with three steaming mugs. We slid into the bench seat opposite her.

"Thanks," I said, dropping the dragon pig beside me. Luckily, the dragon we'd found decided to take the form of a baby pig while it stayed in town. Maybe less luckily, it had decided to stay with me.

I mean, yes, having a dragon had come in handy. Back before the demon Bathin had been dating my other sister, he'd promised me he would save Ryder from a blizzard.

Only problem? He saved him by kidnapping him.

Demons.

On the upside, dragons have the unique ability to find demons no matter where they hide.

So all I'd had to do was tell my little dragon pig to fetch, and off it had popped.

Ryder appeared back home an instant later.

So had the demon.

It had been a weird Christmas.

But even though the dragon pig looked like a piggy, it was a dragon and it could *eat*.

"Mocha?" Jean asked.

"Of course." Frigg had on a soft, wheat-colored sweater that made her long blonde hair shimmer like sunshine. The sweater was nice. I was used to seeing her in her tow company gear: button-down shop shirt with her name embroidered over the pocket.

"Day off?" I guessed.

"Just the morning. There's a storm coming. That means tow jobs." She leaned back against the booth, her arm resting across the top of it.

The dragon pig did a quick little circle before spotting the cutlery on the table. It *oink*ed.

"Spoons later, if you behave," I told it. "Home spoons."

It grunted, a very piggy sound, but a thin tendril of smoke rose from its nostrils.

"Oh, which reminds me." Frigg dug in the backpack next to her and pulled out a handkerchief tied around something that clattered. "Lug nuts," she said. "Broken and rusted."

The dragon pig squeaked. Happy. Very happy.

I untied the kerchief. "Thank you." I plunked the lug nuts down next to the dragon pig, and it went to town, sucking up those hunks of metal.

"So what did you need to see me about?"

"Since you're not on vacation, I thought we might as well do this now. Why aren't you on vacation, by the way?"

Jean snorted, then rubbed whipped cream off her nose. "So many things on her plate. Such a busy woman. Ordinary won't survive if she doesn't babysit."

"I don't babysit," I groused. "I'm the Chief of Police. I protect."

Jean rolled her eyes. "We're fine, Delaney. I don't know how many times I have to say that. We. Are. Fine."

"Here we go!" Piper arrived at our table with a serving tray.

"Did you order for us?" I asked Frigg.

Frigg shook her head. "Why bother when Piper knows what we want anyway?"

Piper blushed, pleased with the compliment. She was a demigod, the only one in town, and her relationship with the gods was sometimes strained.

Her ability to know what someone was going to

order was pretty cool, though. On the table, she placed clam chowder for Jean, a chicken salad for me, and a veggie burger for Frigg.

"How'd I do?" she asked. "Everyone happy?"

"This looks great." Jean and Frigg looked just as satisfied.

Dragon pig stood on its back legs, that little pink curl of a tail wagging like mad. It grunted, a tiny piggy sound, and Piper chuckled. "Of course I didn't forget you."

She placed a folded towel on the table. I lifted the corner and found six broken forks.

"New hire has been a little hard on the cutlery," she said.

A clash and shatter sounded from the kitchen. Everyone in the diner went silent. Heads turned as if they could see the disaster through the walls.

Piper just shook her head. "That's my cue. Excuse me." She spun and was across the room, pulling a bottle of ketchup out of her apron and plunking it down in front of a family of four before she powered into the kitchen.

"Good manners," I told the dragon pig. "No feet on the table."

The dragon pig instantly dropped back onto the seat. I smuggled it a fork, which it chomped down in one bite.

"You were saying?" I asked Frigg.

"I've been storing them for over a year now," she said.

"The god powers?"

DEVON MONK

She nodded, her mouth full of burger.

Jean was taking selfies with a spoon of clam chowder. I stabbed chicken, spinach, and dried cranberry and chewed. "That's long enough," I said. "The hand off to a new keeper shouldn't be hard. Who's up next?"

"That's what I wanted to talk to you about. We've done the full rotation. Every god has covered a year of watching over the resting powers. I think we should give the new guy a crack at it."

Jean stopped posing and tuned back into the conversation. "Really?"

"Than," I said. "You want Death to look after all the gods' powers." It wasn't a question, so Frigg didn't answer it. She just stuck another fry in her mouth.

Oh, this could go wrong. So very wrong. "Okay. I'll talk to him."

"Is that hesitation I hear in your voice? Is there something about Than taking over the powers I should be worried about?"

"Just that this is the first time in his existence he's vacationed."

She did that "maybe" wobble with her hand.

"The first time he's vacationed in Ordinary," I amended.

"True. Don't think he can handle being guardian of the powers?"

"I think he'll do fine. But I want to go over the rules and expectations with him first."

Which meant cancelling another vacation plan. Ryder was going to kill me.

"When did you want to hand them off?" I asked.

18

"Think he can get it all together by this weekend?"

Jean cleared her throat and coughed. It sounded like *vacation*.

"Actually," Frigg said, "Than's a go-getter. Tell him to step it up. Tomorrow morning would be better."

Jean gave her a thumb's up. I just rolled my eyes. "I'll let you know if he's ready by then."

"Works for me. Where are you going on vacation, anyway?"

I stabbed at a piece of romaine, the tines crunching and snapping the spine of the leaf, as I imagined every person who had asked me that over the last month.

"Somewhere outside Oregon," Jean said. "Right? That pretty bed and breakfast?"

"We haven't decided yet. We have deposits on a couple places, and Ryder has a pile of backups if those fall through." I stuffed salad in my mouth and wished the carrots and celery were loud enough to drown out the questions I knew they were about to ask.

Why haven't you gone yet? Is it because of the upcoming wedding? Are you and Ryder okay? What's wrong?

I didn't want to answer any of those things. Not after months of it. Because nothing was wrong. It was just Ordinary being Ordinary, and me trying to keep it safe.

"You know," Frigg said, picking up on my mood. "There are many beautiful and interesting places in the world. Sometimes letting fate take the reins will put you on the best path."

"Road trip," Jean said. "Hell yeah. Just flip a coin at

every intersection. Heads, right, tails, left, show up wherever you arrive."

"What if I want to go straight ahead?" I asked.

Frigg lifted her burger, tucking some of the onions back between the buns. "Then just commit to the decision. *Stop* worrying." Her gaze met mine, her eyes sharp with something that made me feel like she was looking a lot deeper into me than I wanted. "And go."

She took a huge bite of the burger, and I wondered if that was the solution. Just *go*.

Could it be that easy?

My phone pinged. Ryder again.

I'll take that as a no.

I didn't text back.

The phone pinged.

Let's talk tonight at home. Ok?

Really, he'd been more than patient.

I texted: *Have to see Than. Will be home later.*

Did you feed the dragon pig?

It had a snack.

He sent a thumbs up and a heart.

I sent three hearts and a kissy face.

"I've got this one." Jean's fingers and thumb flew over her phone.

"Problem?"

"I don't think so. Hatter just texted that there was a complaint at Mom's Bar and Grill. Something about a stripper? Gonna make sure there isn't a problem."

More delays. I swallowed a groan. "Fine, let's go."

"No. You," she stood and pointed at me, looking

every inch an officer of the law, "go talk to Than. I'll handle this. Hatter's headed there. Kelby too."

Hatter was a police officer we'd stolen from a town up north, and Kelby was a giantess, who was one of our reserve officers like Ryder and Than. She had a way about her that took the heat out of confrontations and left everyone laughing.

"That's Kelby now." Jean's gaze moved from the widow beside me back to my face. "Look, I know you're worried about stuff. And I know it's been… well, nuts lately."

I stabbed a carrot and shoved it in my mouth.

"But would you just *go* already?" She smiled to soften the words. "I promise you'll have a lot of fun and you'll be so happy you did it."

"Who knows," Frigg added. "You might even relax."

"The horror," Jean said with a grin. "Go. Wherever he picks, just say yes and go."

She turned and jogged out the door before she'd even gotten her coat on and zipped.

Kelby flashed her headlights, Jean ducked into the vehicle, then they pulled a cookie and headed south into town.

I watched the car until I couldn't see it anymore. There were little toys lined up along the windowsill, the plastic ones that ran on solar power. They all seemed to be waving good-bye.

"You want to talk to me about why you're afraid of going on vacation?" Frigg asked.

"When have I said I was afraid?"

She just took another bite of the burger and waited.

"I'm here because you," I held up a fork of spinach and stabbed it toward her, "called me here."

"You've been planning your vacation since November."

"Ever tried to be Chief of Police in this town?"

She shook her head.

"Smart." I chewed the spinach, she went after the burger again, and Willie sang on about being on the road.

"If you want to reschedule this handoff," she said, "I could keep the powers a little longer."

"No, that screws things up. There are rules in place for a reason, and one year is the rule for the powers. I knew it was coming up."

We were quiet for a few more bites. "So Bertie's calling a meeting tonight," I said.

"About the festivals she's planning to throw?"

"You coming?"

"No. Very no. What's the most no?" she asked. "That much no. Doubled."

I laughed. "It's not that bad. She'll listen to suggestions."

"She'll conscript volunteers."

"I'm on the hook no matter what. Don't you want to pitch in a little time for the good of the community?"

"Gee, what would that be like? Good of the community? Would that be like digging tourists' vehicles out of sand banks and sand dunes and the ocean and the lake and the river and off the side of the cliffs and…"

I laughed again. "Point taken. But if you ever get tired of dragging people out of ditches, I'm sure Bertie would have a delightful concession stand or sweaty, costumed mascot position for you."

"Nope. I'll leave the festivals and events to the Valkyrie. I'm happy in the ditches."

The dragon pig *oink*ed, tired of being ignored, so I fed it a couple more forks while we finished our meal.

I picked up the tab, Frigg said she'd catch the next one, then she headed to the door. Before she opened it, she turned, hand on the bar.

"Oh, and Delaney?"

"Yes?" I left money on the table, scooped up the dragon pig, and headed for the coat rack.

"Take some time off. You, of all people, have earned it." She pulled the hood of her coat over her head and sauntered out into the rain, slow and easy as a summer day.

CHAPTER THREE

Ryder texted two more times: *rentable teepee*, and *bungee jumping.*

I laughed at that last one because jumping off cliffs wasn't my idea of relaxation.

I sent him a smiley face, then pulled up to Than's house. The shades were drawn. I didn't see any light peaking around the edges.

"What do you think?" I asked the dragon pig, lying in the passenger seat.

The windshield wipers were going full tilt. Even though the car was idling, it wasn't enough to keep the rain from blurring up the world.

"Doesn't look like he's home."

Dragon pig had curled up in the seat, happy and full of forks. It ignored me, both eyes closed, a tiny little snore rumbling in its chest.

"Let's give him a call." I thumbed through my contacts and dialed.

"Reed Daughter." Than's voice was smooth and

cool, like I'd just interrupted important reading.

"Hey," I said. "I need to discuss something with you. Are you home?"

"Why would I be there?"

I glanced at the dash. Three o'clock.

"I just thought business might not be booming at your kite shop."

The wind punched the Jeep in the side, rocking it. Sheets of rain slashed sideways through the air.

"Oh?"

"It's a little weather-y for kites today."

There was a pause. Then, "I am aware. Is this what you wish to discuss? The weather?"

"No. I was…. You know what? Never mind. You're at your shop? Can I meet you there?"

"I am open until four p.m." He hung up.

Still hadn't quite nailed the social norms of the phone call. I tipped my phone down. "Okay, then. I'll see you there. Coffee would be great." I put the Jeep in gear and backed out of the dead end next to his house. "Cookies too? You're too thoughtful."

The dragon pig snorted. It sounded like a tiny grumbly laugh.

"You're staying in the car, bucko."

All I got for that was louder, more dragon-y snorts.

The drive wasn't far, but the weather was getting worse. Tough shore pines swayed in the gale. Softer firs and hemlock boughs whipped and bent. Rain rattled and hushed with the surging wind, turning the Jeep into an amateur drum-line jam session.

Than's kite shop, the tailwind, was a little A-frame

building lit by a nearby shepherd's crook streetlamp. There were no cars in the parking lot, but the shop windows were filled with brightly colored kites. The light inside the shop poured through all that ripstop nylon, turning the windows into stained glass.

I parked as close to the door as was legal and shut off the engine.

"You going to be okay out here?"

The dragon pig opened one eye, and it flashed a deep, burning red.

"Oh, that's right. You're actually a big ol' bad dragon. But look at these soft piggy ears and this squishy pink nose and those sweet piggy eyes."

The dragon pig growled, a very dragon sound.

I chuckled and scratched behind its adorable soft ears. "Okay. If you want to go home, you can pop on outta here. But no eating the car." I put my fingers on the handle. "Or the house. Or anything in the house." Before I opened the door, I added, "You know the rules. Stick by them, and I'll let you slurp down a roll of old chain-link fencing later. Deal?"

The dragon pig flipped on its back, showing its little round belly. Its tiny feet pointing straight up, flopped ears, round nose, and piggy eyes were all very convincing.

I patted its belly. "Good dragon. See you soon."

I shoved out into the rain and wind and storm.

The Open sign on the door was hand-lettered in gold and, really, quite lovely. Death had good penmanship.

A jaunty bell jingled as I stepped into the shop. The

warmth of the place and the soft gold light folded me away from the storm outside. I leaned back against the door, suddenly safe in this little colorful nest inside the roaring storm. Even the clawing of rain on the windows sounded cozy. Like someone should be pouring chocolate and wearing thick socks.

Music played a deep jazzy bass, the tune soft and swanky. Nina Simone was singing about a new dawn and new day. Feeling good.

Death liked blues.

"Than?" I called out, not seeing him in the open space. Well, open was relative. The walls and ceiling were crowded tip-to-tail with kites of every color and whimsy.

Deltas, diamonds, cellular, rokkakus, stunt kites in every color and style. Lofted against the ceiling was a fantasyland of creatures and things: giant squid, koi, a tractor, frogs, a line of cutesy dragons.

Just when I made out one animal (a sheep) another leered behind it (a wolf). The placement was clever but startling, always a predator just around the corner, always some kind of death or danger with each combination.

The longer I looked, the creepier it felt to have all those eyes and teeth shining down on me.

The horror was subtle, but shocking. As if the entire sky above me was alive with chase and capture and flight, with wing and claw and joy…

…that got eaten.

I had no idea how he had repeat customers. Because it sure wasn't that huge sign out front that looked like a clown had carved it with a dull meat clever that brought 'em in.

"Would you care for tea, Reed Daughter?"

I looked down from a spider kite perched so near a shy little ladybug kite that I wanted to smack it with a broom.

Than stood in the now-open door that led to the back room. He had on a chunky cream-colored sweater and a pair of jeans tucked into bright yellow rubber boots with little blue turtles on them.

I'd never seen him in jeans. He was more of a slacks and cheesy, touristy T-shirt kind of guy. The kind of guy who only looked comfortable in a tuxedo, or three-piece suit, and therefore hadn't quite gotten the hang of casual wear.

But here he was looking... well, the rubber boots were ridiculous... but other than that, he looked passably human.

It was shocking. I wasn't sure what I should even say. Maybe he wasn't feeling well. Was this how death got the blues?

"Delaney?" he asked into my silence, his expression entirely blank.

Well, not entirely. No matter how dour and indifferent he tried to be, there was something alive in his eyes. An intelligence, a keen curiosity.

Life. There was a life in his eyes that was ancient and paradoxical, considering what power he had carried for æons.

"Tea," I said, picking up the conversation where I'd dropped it. "Yes. Thank you."

His eyebrows rose, and those sharp eyes sparked with interest. "Come this way."

Said the spider to the fly.

I followed him behind the counter and through the door into an office and storage space. There was a door to one side with a Bathroom sign, and a back door for deliveries. A very small sink was tucked into one corner. A roll-top secretary's desk stood in the other corner, opposite the sink. On the desk was a tiny, stuffed Grim Reaper, big emerald eyes and stitched smile fixed forward, hands clasped around a wee scythe.

"Aw," I said, heading for the stuffy. "It's a little you."

He settled on one of the tall stools near a shelf full of stacked boxes.

"Did you buy this?" I picked it up, mesmerized by the huge eyes.

"No." He sipped tea, and I gave the toy a squish before setting it back in its place.

"Let me guess. Jean?"

"She said it was a housewarming gift."

I pursed my lips but couldn't hold back the grin. "This, I notice, is not your house."

"Yes, well, it is better kept here."

I had no idea why, until I thought back to his house, which I'd only been inside of twice. He had a good eye for decor. Very clean and classy and comfortable. I hadn't seen anything resembling a toy in his home. There wasn't really room for them among all the plants, flowers, bushes, and succulents he had draped—growing and flourishing—in his living room and kitchen.

Death, or at least Death on vacation, had quite the

green thumb. But for some reason he didn't want anyone to know about it.

"Tea?" I asked.

He gestured toward the cup sitting on a side table set up with a burner, tea pot, and a selection of teas.

I poured sugar and cream into the cup and sipped. It was light, creamy, and tasted of spring.

"Why don't I drink tea more often?" I murmured as the music changed to a new song. This one was newer and more upbeat. Pretty sure it was Taylor Swift talking about calming down.

"Did you come to discuss my opinion of your terrible tea-drinking habits?" He hadn't moved, was still on that stool, watching me, the tea a shield between us.

"Nice jeans," I volleyed. "Totally go with the boots."

He paused, then set his cup down on the shelf behind him.

"I understand denim trousers are very 'Pacific Northwest,'" he said.

"Oh, they are. But so is the lumberjack look. Have you thought about flannel and suspenders? Maybe a beard and a beanie?" I tipped my head to one side. "Can you even grow a beard?"

"I can grow whatever facial hair I desire," he said, clearly affronted. "However, if you came here this afternoon to discuss my wardrobe, I would remind you that this is a place of business, not an episode of a fashion show."

I blinked. Because half of that comment was what I'd expected he'd say. But the other half was blowing my mind.

"Please tell me you watch fashion shows. Do you like the wedding dress shows more than the runway designer shows? No! You like that new one that's all about thrift shopping for a look. You do, don't you? That's why you're wearing jeans and turtle boots." I sucked in a big, fake gasp. "You thrift-shopped."

"Denim," he corrected, "because it is practical in this community. Boots," he pointed one long finger downward, "because it is raining." His finger swung to the windows behind me. The sky had darkened another notch, the clouds and storm growing into a real force.

"And the fashion shows?" I wheedled.

"If that is all, I am very busy, Reed Daughter."

The song wound down, Tay Tay telling us all to calm down. I made a big show of looking out into the shop, craning my neck to see the corners. "*So* many customers in here today. You really are super busy. Maybe I should stay to help you keep up."

I thought, just for a moment, that maybe I'd pushed my luck a little too far. He gave me a withering glare, then picked up his tea and sipped again, looking as if he had all the time in the world to watch me rattle on.

"Unless you're rearranging your ceiling menagerie? I'd be happy to help you hang some poisonous jellyfish on top of kitten kites, or whatever other childhood joy you'd like to ruin." I gave him a big grin, letting know I was teasing, but those eyes.

Those eyes were watching me.

"Tell me," he said.

"Tell you what?"

"Who is bothering you and why you are avoiding them."

"Nothing's wrong. No one is bothering me."

He raised an eyebrow. "You have my punch card still?"

"Yes. If I needed you to help with something… big, I'd ask."

"You are telling me there is nothing going on you need help with?"

"There's always something going on," I said. "This is Ordinary and there are no days off. Not really. It's just magic, explosion, curse, monster. All. The. Time."

He sipped tea again, waiting.

"Have you seen anyone with a stolen traffic light?"

One eyebrow twitched "No. If I had, I would have apprehended them, since I am still a reserve officer."

"I know. Well, there's a light missing, so keep your eyes out. Also, I was just talking to Frigg. She's ready to transfer the powers to the next god to take over guarding duties. We've been through the rotation of gods in town. Next up on the list is you."

"I see."

"You can refuse, but if you do, I'll expect you to do it next year. Unless you leave town, there will be no getting out of it."

"I see."

"You'll need some kind of vessel to keep them in. Crow uses the old glassblowing furnace. Odin has a growler. Frigg keeps them in her grove."

"I see."

I gave him a few moments to say something else or

to ask questions. When he remained silent, I pushed on. "If you pick up the job, we'll need to get together with Frigg tomorrow before noon. Will that be enough time for you to decide on your storage vessel?"

His eyes cut sideways to the secretary desk, then returned to me. "Yes."

"Are you agreeing to guard the powers?"

He drew himself up, squaring his shoulders and raising his chin so he could look down his nose at me. I had to admit he looked very regal and imposing. Too bad there was a giant flower-shaped kite on the shelf behind him. The yellow petals fanned out behind his head and spiked down his shoulders like an Elvis impersonator's cape.

"Of course."

Just like that: *of course.*

"Good," I said. "Do you need any help setting up the vessel?"

"I shall need to use a small portion of my power to create it."

I nodded. "That's the one time gods are allowed to use their powers while on vacation. Make the vessel, and make sure it will last until the next time you'll be asked to guard the powers. When you leave Ordinary, you'll want it to go into stasis until you return. No matter how many hundreds of years that might be."

"I understand. I have read all of Ordinary's rules and regulations. You insisted on it."

"Okay then." I gulped down the rest of the cooling tea. "That's decided. See you tomorrow, late morning." I started toward the interior of the shop but heard him moving behind me.

"Are you sure that is all, Reed Daughter?"

Ever since I'd first met him in the casino coffee shop, he'd called me by that name. Ever since then, I'd been telling him that Delaney was fine. More than fine; preferred.

But as the months went by, I realized I kind of liked it. Liked being reminded of my bloodline, my family history.

The Reed family alone had been chosen by the gods to keep Ordinary safe. It was an amazing honor and something that humbled me. It was also something that defined me, just as it had defined my father and our ancestors before us.

Could I leave this place behind, even for a much-needed vacation?

"Ryder wants to get out of town," I said, my back still toward him, as if not facing him would somehow help me get this off my chest.

He just made a soft *hmmm* sound.

"I know it makes sense. To get away. To take a break. My job here is…" I held up my hands, trying to encompass it all. "My job is my life. It's everything I've ever wanted to be. It's everything I want to do. But it is full time. More than. And things have been more difficult since Dad died.

"But if I leave…." I scrubbed at my forehead, then let my hands drop.

"If you leave?" Than repeated.

"Every time I try, something goes wrong. What if

that's fate or destiny or something telling me I shouldn't go? Telling me Ordinary needs me to stay, to put out the fires, to keep the town going forward?

"What if I'm not here to save someone? I don't think… I'd never forgive myself if something happened."

The last came out a little quieter. I hadn't meant to say it all. But it was good to have it out. I just wasn't sure Than was the best counsel on matters like this. He was Death, after all, and dying couldn't possibly bother him as much as it bothered me.

"Is that all, Reed Daughter?" He'd lowered his voice to match mine, his words soft and sanded, smooth and inviting.

"I'm not being a martyr about this. I want to go. But is now the right time? Is now the best time?"

The silence would have been complete, but wind-driven rain shucked down the windows like carwash jets on full blast.

"Delaney."

I held my breath a moment, then, finally, turned.

Than stood in the doorway to the back room, his hands folded in front of him.

"You are worried about Ordinary?"

No, I wanted to say.

"Yes."

"You are worried you will not be here to… save someone from… something?"

I shrugged. When he put it that way, it sounded kind of dumb.

"A lot of people have been hurt. Some have died," I said.

He shifted, just slightly, like a hunter scenting prey. "So this is about trust."

"No." But maybe it was. Trusting my town to look after itself without me. Trusting my gut to make a selfish choice for myself alone and sticking to it.

"Ordinary is what I am. I don't do…" I waved at the windows, at the world beyond Ordinary's borders. "…all that other life out there."

He let the rain and wind fill the space between us, his vision cast over my shoulder, out into that storm, out into that raging world.

"What does your heart tell you?" he asked. Still not looking at me. Still entranced by the violent beauty raging around us.

"My stupid heart wants to be with Ryder no matter what. But I don't even know what kind of person I am if I'm not working."

"Ah."

The rain washed across the window again. Gusts buffeted the little A-frame, which stood steady and strong.

There was something hypnotic about the storm, about the warmth and color of this little room, this hidden gem, floating safely here in the center of such fury and rage.

There was something hypnotic about the god before me too. He hadn't moved, hadn't twitched a finger, hadn't blinked, but I could tell he was waiting for me to think this through. To come to a reasonable conclusion.

I thought there might be some kind of metaphor I was missing. Something about the darkest day still holding a tiny spark of warmth and light.

Something about friends being all one needed when facing a storm.

"These matters," Than said, "are complicated. What solution will you apply?"

"Right now I'm just trying to put out fires so I can say yes. Really say yes without worrying about it."

"Into that 'other life out there'?"

"Yeah. Vacation. I want to go. But Ordinary keeps pulling me back."

"Of course it does."

"Of course?"

"You are a part of it. A part of this land's earth and stone. It will always draw you back."

"Terrific."

"Are you asking my advice?"

Was I? "I think I shouldn't ask you to solve my problems."

"And yet," he said, his hands spreading out in front of him, palms upward. "Here we are, you and I."

The suffering on his face made me smile. "Okay," I said, "I'm game. What would you do if you were in my shoes?"

"I would not go on vacation."

My heart sank. "Really? Why?"

"In my experience, one's peaceful vacation time will be taken up by persons complaining about having to take time away with the one they love. Having to live life."

He delivered it so cooly, so drolly, that it took me a minute. And then I couldn't help it—I gasped. "Did you just throw me some shade? That was me you were talking about in that hypothetical vacation, wasn't it? Did you just tell me I'm being a drama queen?"

"You have an overzealous imagination." He strode past me toward the door. I didn't know that I could be more impressed with a non-answer that simultaneously answered everything I'd asked.

"You really shouldn't make a habit of giving people life advice," I noted as I followed him.

"I shudder to think I would ever desire to do so." He flipped the Open sign to Closed and put his hand on the door handle. "Will you stay for more tea?"

"No thanks," I said. "I'll see you tomorrow?"

"Where shall we meet?"

"It depends. Where are you going to store the powers? At home? Here in your shop? Somewhere else around town?"

He paused. I could almost see the calculations flashing behind his blank expression. "Will Frigg accompany you?"

"Yes."

"Here, then. I will see you here in the late morning."

"Good. Great. I'll be here before noon. Can't wait."

He nodded, just once, in that way he did that almost looked like a bow. "Are you prepared?"

"For?"

"The storm," he said.

A chill ran down my skin, prickling on little feet across the nape of my neck. "What storm?" I knew there was a demon king who wanted to get inside Ordinary. All signs pointed toward war. Did Than have information about that? What if the demon was waiting for me to leave to attack?

Than rolled his eyes. "The weather, Reed Daughter." Rain buffeted the glass. Wind snapped and bit.

"Right," I said, "that storm." I zipped my coat, pulled up the hood and snapped the neck close under my chin. "Yes. Totally ready for it. See you tomorrow."

I took a step, expecting him to open the door, but instead he said, "Delaney?"

"Yeah?"

"It is always best to follow one's heart in these circumstances."

"Leave town no matter how bad things are?"

"Is that what your heart wants to do?"

"Yes. No. Yes."

"There you are," he intoned like it was the best advice ever given.

"And for your information," he added, "I would be an outstanding counselor for anyone's life. I am Death, after all. I know how it all ends."

With that, he opened the door, and the big bad storm huffing and puffing outside rushed inside, catching and clawing at the bright bits of fabric, twisting and turning the jungle canopy of creatures above us, wild and reckless and fierce.

He pressed his blunt, boney fingers into my shoulder and gave me a little push out the door. I opened my mouth to say something, but there was a lot of rain slapping me in the face, so I took the high road.

I fled to the Jeep and ducked in quick. Dragon pig was nowhere to be seen which meant it had popped back home. I didn't blame it. There was a cozy gas fireplace, an overly friendly dog, and a pile of toys it had gathered for its hoard. A much nicer place to weather the storm than in the cold front seat of the Jeep.

I pushed back my hood and grabbed the towel I kept in the glove box. I wiped my face, then paused. Something was different. Something about the shop.

I didn't turn over the engine yet since I wasn't sure what had snagged my attention. I scanned my surroundings, starting with my rearview mirror. No one and nothing in my back seat. No one around the vehicle. The parking lot was empty. The shop was still glowing like it was lit from the inside by Christmas lights.

But something. Something was different.

The creep of evening rubbed the details off the bushes, trees, and other buildings in the area. If it were just a little brighter out, I was sure I'd be able to see what was bothering me.

Then it hit me. The light—or rather, the lack of it. It was darker outside than when I drove up. And not just because of the thickening clouds and setting sun.

The light pole was missing.

There should be a shepherd's crook light pole on the corner near the shop. It had been there when I drove up. I narrowed my eyes and stared at where the light post should be.

Nothing.

Was it raining hard enough to obscure the light post or was the light itself shorted out?

"Dammit." I pulled my hood back on, got out of the Jeep, and jogged to the corner.

Welp. Shorted light wasn't the issue. There was no post there at all. The round metal footing set into the concrete was still there. But the pole and light were gone, leaving a hole in the center of the footing with twisted bits of wire sticking up out of it.

Someone had stolen the light pole.

I turned a full circle. If the thief was in the area, they should be pretty easy to spot. Those light poles were heavy and long. It would take more than one person to move it, and possibly even heavy equipment to remove it from the concrete.

But all I saw was rain.

"Well, hell." I pulled my phone out and took a few quick photos. I didn't want to waterlog the electronics.

Something moved at the edge of my vision, and I spun toward it. A shadow moved about half a block down, but it was impossible to see who or what it might be.

I jogged back to the Jeep, started the engine, and with my lights on, made a quick turn to follow where the shadow had been headed.

There was nothing but rain, houses, bushes, and wind.

CHAPTER FOUR

I DROVE the streets for an hour, looking for any sign of that shadow, or any sign of the missing traffic light or light pole. The list of suspects was growing longer the more I searched.

Who in town was strong enough to rip a light pole out of its base?

Well, since we had an entire family of werewolves in town and a clan of vampires, not to mention most of the mythical or fantastical creatures the stories had ever dreamed up, probably half the town would have the strength or magic to do such a thing.

So maybe a better question was: Who would want to do such a thing? In the middle of a storm with night coming on?

That was where I drew a blank. Infrastructure just wasn't that valuable to any of the people who lived here. I mean, everyone liked having functioning traffic lights and light poles, but no one gained anything from stealing them.

It was possible it was just a prank, a dare. Mrs. Yates' penguin had been stolen on multiple occasions. Enough to grant it its own celebrity status that drew curious tourists into town to take selfies with it.

Those multiple thefts had begun with the high school seniors carrying off a prank.

This was bigger than just a prank.

The dragon pig was a possibility. It ate metal and had gotten its little piggy mouth around a fire hydrant once before we put the kibosh on that.

No, the dragon pig had been following the rules. Plus, a few days ago, we'd let it go to town on an old abandoned school bus on the outskirts of town.

It could be our local kleptomaniac, Bigfoot. But he tended to be nocturnal and wasn't really a thief of all things. More like a sticky-fingered collector of light bulbs.

Light bulbs. Not whole traffic lights and poles. I mean, maybe he was upping his game, but in all the years he'd been in town, he hadn't ever stolen anything bigger than a fluorescent tube. It wasn't his style at all.

So who would need a light that big?

I had no idea. But I knew who I should ask.

I pulled off the street and texted my sister, Myra.

Where you at?

It only took a moment before she replied.

Library. Why?

Need to talk to you.

About your vacation?

I sighed. *Work. The string of thefts.*

We have a string of thefts?

43

We do now.

I'll put on the coffee.

Be there in ten.

When Dad died, he'd left the job of being the Bridge to Ordinary to me. Along with that job came the family library which was the secret location of all the books, spells, scrolls, tablets, and knowledge the Reeds had accumulated over the generations.

I loved the library, but not nearly as much as Myra did. She basically lived and breathed books and scrolls and all magical information.

So Dad had left the library to her, and I couldn't be happier about it.

From the road, the magical library looked like a little pump house set up in the trees. No one really went up here, as it wasn't developed, wasn't good for hiking, and offered no views of the ocean.

And if anyone did happen to wander by, the pump house would be, in fact, a pump house. That was part of the magic of the place.

The only time the big magic was triggered was when Myra visited. She didn't have a key to the library, she *was* the key.

She also had the family gift of being in the right place at the right time. Which was why I wasn't at all surprised that the moment I drove up and parked the Jeep on one side of the mossy stones that acted as a gateway to the pump house/library, Myra opened a door.

Even in the rain, even in the ever-dimming light, it

was magical to see an entire building manifest around her as she stepped out onto the covered front step. The library looked like several fairytale wooden cabins stuck together, all peaked roofs and multi-pane windows.

The light behind her was bright and welcoming. I ducked out of the Jeep and sprinted to the overhang of the step.

"Hey," I said, dripping and cold, the wind shoving me sideways. "Can I come in?"

Myra was off duty today and was wearing a red sweater and black polka-dot leggings. Her rockabilly hair was pulled back with a simple black bow headband. Her eyeliner was winged away from her light blue eyes, making them even wider.

The library didn't allow anyone over the threshold unless Myra permitted it. To date, she'd only allowed me, Jean, and for some reason beyond me, Than, into this treasure trove of information. She hadn't even allowed Bathin in, and he was the demon she was dating.

"Yes, you are welcome here tonight. Get in." She tugged on my shoulder.

I yelped as I basically tripped over the threshold. She shut the door behind me.

The main room was wall-to-wall bookshelves, crowded from floor to ceiling with every kind and style of book imaginable. A flicker of spirits and sparkles of magic floated and peeked between bindings, shimmering in the ragged shadows of spines.

Several ghost-like spirits of the library's volumes

were hanging out here, as they usually did. A young boy lay sprawled on the floor, his head resting on a big, ghostly wolf behind him. Two regally dressed men sipped tea in the corner, leaning close to each other with secret smiles. A woman with a battle axe across her shoulder was throwing dice with an elfin creature and a cat in a top hat. Near the stairwell, a lizard made of blue fire ate berries out of a selkie's fingers.

All of them ghostly. All of them spirits of the books held safe in this space.

I heard several disembodied voices murmur, "*Welcome,*"

"*Delaney,*"

"*Bridge,*"

"*Eldest,*" as the magic of the books recognized me.

"Delaney Reed," a strong male voice said. "How good to see you."

I looked toward the kitchen area.

Harold stood there, smiling. He was much more solid than any of the other book spirits and looked like Cary Grant, suit and all. He used to be an index in the Library of Alexandria. As luck had it, he'd been thrown away, rescued from the fire, and was now caregiver to both the Reed magic library and the magical Reed responsible for it.

"Hi, Harold," I said.

"Would you care for coffee and cookies?"

It felt like I'd been eating and drinking non-stop, but it was still cold and wet out. Coffee equals good. "Yes, please."

"Excellent. And you, Myra? Tea?"

"I'll have coffee too."

His eyebrows went up and so did mine. Myra was a tea lover through and through.

"He made chocolate, chocolate-chunk, extra-fudge cookies," she explained. "Coffee's gonna go great with that."

"Will you be in the sitting room?" he asked.

Myra smiled at him. "Upstairs, yes. Thank you."

"Carry on. I'll be up in a moment."

I pulled off my coat and hung it to drip on the coat rack behind the door. My phone in the coat pocket vibrated, so I pulled it out and glanced at the screen.

Ryder.

Dinner? Promise no more brochures.

No more than a dozen?

He sent a smile face, an angel, and a globe. Then: *Don't forget it's your day to feed the dragon pig.*

I sent a thumbs up and stuck the phone in my pants pocket. I'd need to go pick up that rusted fence Aaron was holding for me.

"Thefts?" Myra led the way across the room to the stairs and started up.

"You know about the missing traffic light?"

"Yeah. Jean told me this morning."

"Now the light pole outside Than's kite shop is gone."

She slowed and glanced back over her shoulder. "The light pole."

"The light pole."

She raised her dark eyebrows and took the last few steps to the upper level, heading straight to the sitting room, which was really more of an inviting little space with soft couches and a clutter of loose-leaf letters and booklets scattered on shelves and small tables.

She took the couch. I flopped down into the comfy chair across from her, the wooden coffee table, polished to a deep shine, between us.

"Did Than report it?" she asked.

"No, I was there. Frigg wants to transfer the powers and it's his turn."

"Well, that's gonna be fun to watch. So you noticed the pole missing?"

"It was there before I went in and when I left, it was gone."

"You didn't hear anything?"

"Storm."

She nodded. "All right, talk me through it."

It wasn't a long story, but I recited everything that had happened and pulled up the photos on my phone.

"Who would want a streetlight?" she asked.

"That's why I'm here."

Harold came in with a tray holding two coffee mugs and a plate of small, chocolatey cookies.

"Thanks," I said. "Are you going to join us?"

"As much as I like a good mystery," he smiled, "and I certainly do, there seems to be a discrepancy in the inventory I am excited to ferret out."

He walked out of the room. I threw Myra a look.

"What are *you* missing?"

"Not streetlights. It's just a book that isn't on the shelf where it's supposed to be. It's still in the building," she said before taking a huge bite of cookie. "We'd know if it were really gone."

From the room below came a *thunk* followed by a laugh. Harold's voice floated up from the living area. "William, Dashiell, what have I told you about lobbing volumes at Edgar? Pick that up and help me find your missing shelf mate."

There was another *thunk* and the fast tap of shoes running.

Myra just rolled her eyes. "Books."

I tried the cookie. "These are fantastic."

"He found the recipe on the internet." She grinned. "He's determined to find the best version of every kind of cookie, no matter where he has to go to get the recipe."

"Good man." I washed the chocolate down with a gulp of coffee. "Light post."

"Well, there's Bigfoot," she said. "He loves light bulbs."

"I thought about that. Has he ever escalated to this level before?"

"No. Not that I know of."

"So we can talk to him, but it's not really his M.O."

"Is it possible we have another dragon loose in town? It could have taken the shape of anything it wanted to be. Now it's eating metal?"

"Possible. I'll ask dragon pig to look for it. But both items are big public lights. If a dragon wanted to eat metal, there is more easily accessed metal objects in town. Park benches, garbage cans…"

"… fire hydrants," she added.

"Yep. Not to mention cars and sheds and fencing. And since nothing else metal has been reported missing, I'm thinking dragon number two isn't our suspect."

"Worth asking about."

"I will."

She finished off her cookie and pulled her coffee mug into her hands. "It's not like they're easily sold or shipped. Can't strip them down for anything valuable."

"Copper wire?"

"Not enough to make it worth the effort. That shadow you saw out by Than's shop. How big was it?"

"Hard to say. Bigger than a human, I think."

The problem with that was we had leshiye and giants and all manners of larger supernaturals in town. To live among the non-magic humans, many of the big supernaturals carried a spell to change their appearance, or otherwise used their powers and abilities to make people see them as something that fit in with the common world.

"It's early to rule out humans, but let's do it for a moment and think through who would want a light pole so bad they'd steal it in the middle of a storm," she said.

"All right. Any of the gods could be behind it."

"They can't use their powers."

"Sure, but there's still magic, and any one of them can use magic."

"You think one of the gods, here in town, on vacation, is going to be dumb enough to steal traffic lights just for kicks?"

"Well, Crow, maybe."

She grinned. "Did you stop by his garage sale?"

"That tent," I said. "You?"

"Yeah. Didn't see traffic lights."

"Was anything else...strange about his sale?" I asked. "Other than the lurid pink whale?"

"Spill it," she said. "Whatever you just thought of."

"There was an old record player and records. I thought I saw a shine of magic on them. Maybe."

"Shine?"

"Just a soft gold glow. Might not be anything."

"Might be a dragon," she said.

"Or a spell? There was more than one shiny moment."

"Why would a record player need a spell?" she asked.

I shrugged. "Too many possibilities. Crow got the stuff from abandoned storage units. I should pull records to find out who owned them. Maybe that would give us an idea about the record player. If it's magic."

"Did someone buy it?"

"Couple of the ladies from the knitting club."

"This is important?"

"Isn't it?"

"Okay, so let me get this straight." She tucked one bare foot up under her on the couch. "You are going to pull storage records, track down the knitting club members to see if a record player is magic, and tell the dragon pig to search the town for other dragons. You are also, simultaneously going to solve the thefts and transfer god powers to Death, who hasn't ever looked after the powers in Ordinary."

"Yes?"

She stared at me for an extended moment. "LaPine is beautiful this time of year."

I frowned. "What does that have to do with anything?"

"I've talked to Ryder."

Everything in me stilled. "Okay?"

"He said you've shot down every idea he's come up with."

"That's not true."

She tipped her head down, eyebrow raised.

"Some of the ideas I haven't said yes or no to yet. I like them, I just keep getting called away by things and don't want him paying cancellation fees."

"You're avoiding leaving town."

"Hey, so here's a fun question," I said brightly. "How's it going with *your* boyfriend? Has the demon earned the right to come inside the secret library?"

She rolled her eyes. "Bathin and I are doing just fine, thank you. I am perfectly comfortable with not letting him into the library yet, and you know what? So is he. Because this is a place full of old magics, and I'm the one keeping them safe and secure. Also, that's not what we should be talking about."

"Well, neither is my relationship."

She blew air through her lips. "For someone who has been in love with a person for most of her life, you are the slowest person to commit to anything new."

"Slow? The moment he proposed to me, I said yes."

"After the demon showed up."

"Yeah, there was that."

"After we talked you out of going after said demon to take care of business while poor Ryder was still on his knees."

"He wasn't on his knees," I mumbled into my cup. "He tackled me."

She settled back, waiting for more. Waiting for the truth.

"We have a string of thefts, a god power exchange, and a Valkyrie on the hunt for fresh volunteer blood, and you think I should just drop all that and leave town?"

"Dad was like that."

"I know.

"Never wanted to leave."

"I know."

"Workaholic."

"I'm not Dad."

"But you're making the same choices he made."

"Maybe it's a Bridge thing?" I mused.

"I think it's a you-don't-trust-us thing."

"Whoa. Not true."

"You don't trust us to look after ourselves and each other while you're gone."

"I trust you. Most of you. Not Crow…"

"You think something bad is going to happen, something terrible, and you won't make it back in time to save us."

That was so close to the heart, I choked on coffee, my throat too tight to work correctly.

"You know Jean will tell us if something really bad is going to happen," Myra went on unflappably. "She's been practicing being more sensitive to her gift, to give us longer warning times before doom hits."

"I know."

"You know if something terrible happened, all the gods in this town would rise up and kick ass, even though that means they'd have to pack up their powers and leave town for at least a year. They've done it before."

"And they loved it so much last time. We didn't suffer for that at all."

"They took it pretty well."

"Thor was so bitchy it rained all summer."

"Thor's always bitchy."

I hummed in agreement and took another sip. "Jean got hit by a car."

"I remember."

"You started dating a demon."

"Which was nothing like getting hit by a car."

"He broke your heart."

"And my heart mended, just like Jean's bones mended. But what about you?"

"What about me?"

"Have you mended from all those hits? All the things that have happened to us? To Ben, Old Rossi, Ryder? All the things that have happened to you?"

"I'm fine." It came out stiff, stilted. It came out hard,

because all those memories crowded in, all those failures, all those fears.

All the times I'd failed the people in my town were still back there, somewhere in my mind, screaming warnings that it could happen again. That I could fail again.

"Delaney," she said, soft but determined, knowing me too well, knowing me as only a sister could. "None of those things would have turned out any differently. We made our choices with the best information we had at the time.

"We've won, and we've lost. But we're here, together. Even if it were legal to turn back time for a do-over, would you really want to make different choices?"

I cleared my throat. "I might."

She gave me a level stare. "And if you did, do you think the outcome would be any better?"

"Maybe," I said. "Maybe Ryder wouldn't be the vassal to a petty god. Maybe I wouldn't have lost my soul for a year. Maybe you wouldn't have had your heart broken, and Jean wouldn't feel like she had to get better at her gift just because she almost didn't know the big troubles were coming until they hit."

"Or maybe we would be right here, you and I, drinking coffee in a winter storm, trying to figure out who's developed an industrial light fetish, and arguing over your inability to let go for a few days. Also," she added, "eating really good cookies."

I inhaled, exhaled. "They are really good." I plucked another off the plate and popped the whole thing in my mouth. "How about this? I promise if I get the powers safely in Than's hands, I will pack my bags and flee tomorrow. Before the next problem hits."

She tipped her head to one side, then shrugged. "Will you promise me you will let go and have fun?"

"Yes?"

"Will Ryder?"

"I think he's more than willing to let go. Have you seen him after a few beers?"

"The dancing," she breathed.

"So white guy," I agreed.

She grinned. "He knows how to have fun. I think he needs time away from this town too. You both need time away from your job and his job, and family and friends, and just... everything. He saw you get shot, Delaney. He saw you lose your soul. He saw you die. Was right here for all of it."

"I was only dead for a minute."

"Try telling Ryder it wasn't a lifetime."

I wasn't dumb enough to tell Ryder that. We didn't talk much about all the bad stuff. Not because we didn't have time to rehash everything, but because we both understood that those things were a part of being the Bridge to Ordinary, a part of being the police chief.

I was going to take some hits.

It was my honor to make sure everyone was safe, to make Ordinary welcoming for people and beings of all manner of existence. I was proud of our little town. Proud of the people and supernaturals and others who made it their home.

Ryder knew my job was a part of me, as vital as the breath in my lungs.

But yeah. Getting away from this place was beginning to take the top slot in my genie-three-wish fantasies.

"Tomorrow," I said. "I'm on vacation."

"Promise?"

"Promise."

My phone buzzed. I glanced at the screen and groaned.

"What?" Myra asked. "Ryder?"

"No. Bertie."

"The planning meeting?"

I tucked my phone in my pocket and leaned my head back against the soft cushion of the chair. "Do you think she'd miss me if I weren't there? Or maybe if I were just dead?"

"Yes. Also if you were on vacation right now, she'd excuse your absence. But look where you are. Here. In the Valkyrie's reach. Stupid."

I groaned again and rubbed my forehead.

Myra stood. "Come on. I'll go with you. You know she'll want all of us to attend."

"Have I told you I love you lately?" I pushed up onto my feet.

"Nope," she said. "And that's not going to change my mind about your vacation avoidance."

"Oh my gods," I said, "I'm not avoiding it. I'm *trying* to get out of town."

"I've never seen a Reed woman not get something she sets her sights on."

"Meaning?"

"For someone who says she wants to leave town, you're still right here."

"Don't you have a demon to torment?"

She grinned, and it was wicked. "Yes, but he's not here eating all my cookies."

Just for that, I stole the last three on the plate and stuffed them all in my mouth in one go.

She laughed and strode out the door. "Get going, Chief," she said. "We're burning daylight."

CHAPTER FIVE

"What's with the mallet?" I asked Jean.

My youngest sister shifted the comically huge hammer over her shoulder and gave me wide eyes like she had no idea what I was talking about. "This old thing?"

We were inside the cavernous hall of the community center, which had once been the grade school and was now the office and seat of power for our local Valkyrie. The neatly printed sign on the brick wall stated Meeting with a blocky arrow pointing toward what was once a gymnasium.

Myra ignored us both and strolled off to the meeting.

"Is it a collectable? Like from a movie or something?" I asked.

"Nope. I got it from Crow's sale. Went back after the call to Mom's, and it was there and… I had to have it."

"Like the hippo."

"House hippo," she corrected.

"Which you had to have because…"

"They bring luck."

"And the hammer?"

She started off toward the main room. "I just felt like having it." She paused. "I'm trying to listen to my gut more. Like Myra, you know?"

"Uh-huh. And it was totally your gut that wanted you to have a Harley Quinn mallet?"

"So much gut," she said.

I shook my head but couldn't hide my smile. "You're ridiculous."

She waggled her eyebrows and followed me into the gym.

"Delaney Reed," Bertie snapped as soon as I stepped through the door. "Jean. We've been waiting." Her tone of voice made it sound like she'd been waiting for hours, but I knew the meeting didn't even start for another five minutes.

Still, one does not piss off a Valkyrie if one does not want to be made the tasting judge of every weird cooking contest said Valkyrie dreams up.

Images of the time I'd been roped into judging the Rhubarb Rally flickered behind my eyes, and I shuddered.

Never again.

I scanned the room. Bertie was behind the podium at the front. Folding chairs spread out in an arc before her. She looked like a spry, business-savvy octogenarian, her short white hair choppy and her suit jacket a deep, rich plum.

Her gold fingernails were set off by the hoop

earrings, chunky bracelets, and cascade of jeweled neck-laces she wore. Her eyes were sharp, her make up on point. She posed there, as if perched atop a mountain, scanning the cliffs below for things to kill.

"Sorry to keep you waiting," I said easily. I strolled to the left where Myra already sat, saving three seats, which seemed odd since there was only Jean and me, but I figured someone would be joining us.

She did these sorts of things automatically. All part of her gift. Right place, right time.

Jean eased down to the chair next to Myra, dropped the mallet into the row in front of her, and sat. I took the seat next to her.

The conversations in the room picked up again. I took a little time cataloging who had come out into the teeth of a storm to listen to Bertie list all the festivals and events she was going to drag us through this year.

The lineup didn't change all that often. The people in attendance were humans, gods, and supernaturals—shop keepers, bed and breakfast owners, restaurant managers, the bowling alley guy, and putt-putt golf owner—who all benefited from the tourist traffic the events brought in.

Mixed in with the business owners were folks who headed up local charities, and hobbyists who were also funded by T-shirt, souvenir, and craft sales at their booths. Then there were the usual handful of volunteers who showed up no matter what the event.

Bertie sorted through sheets of paper, then tapped a stack to line up the edges, and walked out from behind the podium.

"Let's pass these out," she said, handing half the stack to a guy named Curt in the first row. He took a sheet and passed the stack to his right. Bertie stalked in front of the gathering, moving to some sort of internal pendulum of her own.

At exactly the top of the hour, she turned and clapped her hands.

"Welcome everyone. I'm pleased to see you've come out today despite the rain, as this is one of the most important meetings I'll be holding this year."

I settled back. This was the same script I'd heard every January meeting for at least a decade.

"Ordinary is renowned for our delightful, entertaining, and charitable community events," she said. "This year, I'd like to mix it up a bit."

Myra leaned toward me and Jean. "Her sister Valkyrie in Boring, Oregon, just announced *her* list of festivals," Myra whispered. She thumbed through her phone screen, then handed it to me.

I read through them. "They're all Bertie's festivals," I whispered back.

Myra nodded.

"Oh, gods," I said. "She stole her festivals. This is going to be a train wreck, isn't it?"

"Chief Reed," Bertie called out. "Did you have a comment you'd like to share?"

"No. Nope." I said. "Just exchanging information on a case. About trains. Uh, wrecking." It was a lie, but luckily no one in the room had the ability to read minds.

Or at least I hoped they didn't.

"When I say mix it up," Bertie said, back on track,

"what I intend is to invigorate Ordinary's offerings. To really create something exciting and new that no one can easily copy or steal.

"The paper you have lists last year's most successful events. To the right of those are my suggested changes. You will note that many of the seasonal events will remain the same structurally but may change in detail or focus. For example, the Rhubarb Rally will now be the Strawberry Jamboree. Many of the same events will be held—the pie contests, canning contests, and, of course, art, but instead of basing the event on rhubarb, we will base it on strawberries. Any questions?"

Curt's hand shot up. "What about all the people who look forward to the Rhubarb Rally? Won't we disappoint them?"

"A very good question. Which is why I'm proposing we run a simultaneous secondary event. An event within an event, if you will. The Rhubarb Rally within the Strawberry Jamboree will feature our traditional rhubarb offerings.

"That is my plan for all of our seasonal events. If we want to keep Ordinary fresh, and keep the tourists coming, we need to reimagine our offerings. Take what works and add a dash of something new to it."

I glanced at Myra and Jean. They both sat there wide-eyed. Shell shocked.

Yep. Making every event a two-in-one was going to be a royal headache for logistics. Not to mention manpower and getting the advertising and marketing correct. I glanced to my right to see how the audience was taking it.

Mixed, but definitely intrigued.

The door opened, and a man paused on the threshold before spotting me. He held my gaze with laser-like focus as he walked down the aisle toward me.

Ryder Bailey was a handsome man. With his light brown hair, mossy eyes, and wide shoulders, he looked every inch a man who worked with his hands and worked hard. I loved the look of him, the strength of his body. But it was that mind of his, clever and thoughtful and curious that really did me in.

And right now, I could almost hear what he was thinking: Why had I'd been avoiding him? Why weren't we on our vacation right now?

I gave him a small smile and pointed at the open chair next to me—thanks, Myra—then turned my attention back to Bertie before she called me out in class again.

Ryder settled into the chair. The scent of rain mixed with the sweet, foresty smell that was all him.

"Hey," I whispered.

"Hey," he whispered back.

I put my hand on his thigh, and he immediately dropped his palm over mine. Our fingers laced together, and his thumb found the inside of my wrist, stroking gently there.

A chill washed over me, and I leaned my shoulder into his, enjoying his weight as he leaned back.

"What'd I miss?" he whispered.

I handed him the paper. He read through it, and his eyebrows knitted. "Huh."

Bertie hadn't missed a beat or stopped talking. She

was still spinning the details of how she was going to merge the Slammin' Salmon parade with something that involved a town-wide, cosplay-treasure hunt, and I was listening. Really, I was.

But only with a part of me, the police officer part of me that was calculating how we'd handle traffic, lost kids, and shoplifting.

The rest of me, the *most* of me, was zeroed in on the pad of Ryder's thumb. The soft stroke across my wrist, over and over, bringing me out of my mind, out of my worries, back again and again to my body. To sitting right here, in this moment, with him.

I felt my shoulders relax, my breathing settle. A soft tingle radiated deep in my belly. This, now, was familiar. A part of my life that I never wanted to change. Both of us together, holding on no matter what ridiculous events were headed our way. Both of us connected, alive.

"Sign-up sheets are here to the right," Bertie called out, "and I strongly encourage each of you to sign up for at least one event. When we all work together, we can make great things happen. Also," she went on before anyone could bolt for the door, "suggestions, comments, and ideas are vital to the success of these events.

"Please do not be shy. Tell me what you think. Tell me what you need or expect from these events, and I will take it into consideration. If anyone would like to discuss something in more depth, I will be here for another hour."

The room filled with conversation, and Ryder turned

toward me. "Wanna sign up now, or after everyone's picked the good stuff?"

"You forget there is no good stuff," Jean said, leaning around me. "What's the latest idea, almost-bro?"

"Cabin in the mountains. Solitude. Quiet. Just the two of us. Snow, fir trees, and a hot tub. Heaven."

"Nice," she said. "Don't you think that's nice, Delaney? Super nice?"

"Super nice," I agreed, meaning it. "Let's sign up. We don't want to miss out on that bowling-league-burger-and-balloon-ride thing."

Jean laughed. "Do you think she'll let us bowl *from* the hot air balloons? Because I am in for it, like a million."

"I think there's a rule about dropping bowling balls out of the sky," I said. "And if there's not, I'm making one."

I was already on my feet, but Ryder stayed sitting for a moment, our hands still clasped.

I glanced down at him. "What?"

A small smile curved his lips, but he just shook his head. "Nothing." He tugged on my hand, once, then made to let go. Suddenly I didn't want that.

"Hey," I said. I leaned down, and he narrowed his eyes.

"What are you up to, future Mrs. Bailey?"

"This." I kissed him, and knew he hadn't expected it, because he tensed up for just a second before his mouth softened and he kissed me back.

This was where I belonged. This was us, together.

And my world, spinning on the axis of us, set everything right, made everything good.

When I pulled away, his eyes were soft. "What was that for?"

"I love you," I said, still not straightening fully, wanting to keep this moment just for us. "You know that, don't you?"

If I hadn't known him for all my life, I wouldn't have noticed the slight hitch in his breathing, wouldn't have noticed the tightening of the skin at the corners of his eyes.

"I do. And I love you too," he said.

I nodded, but that hitch had made my world wobble again. The fear of not being able to get out of town fast enough collided with the fear of not doing my job to keep Ordinary safe. My stomach turned.

"Hey," he said, seeing me as well as I had seen him. "We'll figure it out. It's a vacation, Laney. That's supposed to be a fun thing, remember? No stress."

I nodded, but everything in me tossed and turned, as restless as the January rain.

He stood, keeping our hands together, as unwilling as I to release this connection. "What were you talking to Than about?" he asked, as we joined the line at the sign-up sheets.

"Frigg's ready to pass the baton." Since we were among humans who didn't know about the supernatural people in their town, discretion was necessary.

"Who's next?" he asked. That was something else I loved about Ryder. He had only found out about the magical, godly, supernatural side of Ordinary a couple years ago. But he'd immediately become both wildly curious about it and also wildly protective.

I gave his hand a squeeze. "Than."

"Ah," he said, catching on. "First time, right?"

"Yep."

"Expecting trouble?"

"I don't think so, but well. First time."

"Mmmm," he said. "When?"

"Tomorrow morning."

"All right. Any plans after that?"

"Some things have been stolen and there's something weird about some storage units…"

He raised an eyebrow and just looked at me. It was devastating.

An apology almost escaped my mouth, but I wasn't even sure what I was apologizing for. I couldn't help that I was a required part of the powers being transferred to a new resting place. I couldn't help the thefts or the general town weirdness.

"Dinner?" I asked, holding tight.

"Yes?"

"Did you have something planned?"

"I put something in the oven," he hedged.

"Will it hold?"

"It will. Why?"

"How about you and I do a little romantic stakeout together?"

"You think stakeouts are romantic?"

"If you're with me they are."

For a minute, I thought I'd overstepped. That even mentioning my work—his work, too, since he was a reserve officer—was too much when we'd been trying to ditch this town and flee.

But then a smile brightened his face and put a wicked little gleam in his eye. "Sounds like fun. You going to tell me who we're spying on?"

"It's reconnaissance, not spying. And I think it would be better for you to see it with your own eyes."

CHAPTER SIX

"TRENCH COAT?" Ryder, next to me in the Jeep, asked.

"Bad weather. A trench coat doesn't really stand out."

"With the fedora and black gloves and sunglasses?"

I picked up my binoculars and zoomed in on the suspect who was tromping into the grocery store.

"Okay, yeah. It's a little noticeable."

"I expected more hair," Ryder said, his own binoculars trained on the store.

We both watched as Bigfoot sneezed into the crook of his elbow violently enough to knock his hat off.

"He's wearing the spell necklace," I said.

"What's the spell?"

"Makes him look human to other humans."

Ryder adjusted the focus. "Okay. A very hairy guy, but yeah, I guess I can see it."

"You're more than just human. God-touched," I said. "So you see more than most."

"I see a really tall hairy guy in a trench coat having

an allergy attack."

"Yeah, that's the drawback."

"What?"

"He's allergic to magic."

There was a pause while he digested that. "Bigfoot's allergic to magic?"

"Yeah, and Bigfoot's a family name. His personal name is Flip."

Another, longer pause. "Bigfoot's name is Flip."

"But since he's the only Bigfoot in town, he just goes by the family name."

"So there are more?" Ryder asked. "Bigfoots. Bigfeet?"

"Foots. Yeah. They do a family reunion thing every so many years. Not in Ordinary. This year is the reunion year."

"When?"

"Soon, I think. It's a complicated thing involving moon cycles and hair growth."

He grunted.

"Right around the beginning of the year anyway." I shrugged. "We're in the ballpark."

"All right. And you think he might have taken the streetlight?"

"Honestly, no. It's not like him. Light bulbs, yes. Traffic signals? He's never stolen anything other than bulbs. Why would he start stealing such large, obvious, and expensive things now?"

"For the family reunion? Maybe that's how the Bigfoots show they're successful? Whoever can steal the biggest light wins?"

I chuckled. "He's never said anything about that kind of thing, and Myra's looked through all the records. Stealing traffic signals—for any reason—isn't in them."

"Yeah, well, people can surprise you. The kinds of things they don't want to talk about."

I held my breath for a minute, then lowered my binoculars. "I... should apologize. For avoiding you and avoiding talking about our vacation."

He rested his binoculars on the dashboard. "You've talked about it. I seem to recall a lot of 'Later,' and 'I don't like that one,' and 'It's so busy this time of year.'"

I winced. "Yeah, that's basically what I need to talk about. All my excuses."

I rubbed my sweaty palms on my jeans and licked my lips. I wanted to get this right. I wanted him to know this wasn't about us. Well, it was, but it wasn't about me loving him, because that was solid. I was solid with that. Unshakable.

It was more about me trying to figure out how to let go of my responsibilities. Just for a few days.

"Hey." Ryder's hand landed on the back of my neck, sliding under my long ponytail and gently squeezing the tight muscles there and sending a trickle of heat down my spine. "I love you, you know that, right?" he asked.

I blew out a breath. "I know. I love you too." It came out wooden, like I'd never said it before, like someone else was using my mouth without my consent.

I groaned. "This is not going how I wanted it to go."

His hand stilled. After a heartbeat, two, his palm flexed again, kneading muscle. "Us?" he asked.

I twisted so quickly, his hand dislodged. "No! Not us. We——" I pointed between us, "——we're good. We're going where we want us to go. Right?" I asked, trying and failing to hold his steady gaze. "We're still good?"

His fingertips were back, stroking across my neck, calloused from the build he'd just completed. He'd remodeled a little Tudor style home that had suffered through a parade of owners who all thought bigger and more modern was better. They had 'trend-chased the original design right off a cliff.'

He was an architect, yes, but here in Ordinary, hands-on builds were the bread and butter of his business. Plus, he couldn't keep his mitts off a tool belt if he tried.

"We're good," he said soft and low, enough burr in his voice for me to feel it under my skin, warming me. "But you're still not telling me where you want to go on vacation."

This was it, my chance to tell him how I was really feeling. We were going to be married. I needed to be up front with how I felt and what I needed from him. Just like I expected him to be up front with me.

"I want to go on vacation tomorrow," I said, as evenly as I could. "But I don't know if I can."

He drew his fingertips away. I immediately missed their warmth. "Okay."

I waited for him to say more, for him to ask why. Instead, he just picked up his binoculars and trained them back on the store.

I was sitting right next to him. There couldn't be more than a foot between us. The darkness of night—

hastened by the storm, but always early at this time of year—closed us in. Gave us this intimate space.

And yet, I had never felt farther away from him. I hesitated, then picked up my binoculars and pointed them in Bigfoot's general direction.

"So what's our play?" Ryder asked.

"I think we need to sneak out in the middle of the night before anyone can find me and try to give me some new situation only I can handle."

"With Bigfoot," Ryder said. "What's our play with Bigfoot? He's checking out."

I felt the blood rise to heat my cheeks and adjusted the binoculars. "Okay," I said. "It just looks like groceries in his cart."

"You expected something else?"

"Not really, but then again, I didn't expect to be trailing Bigfoot with my fiancé in the middle of a storm."

"It's an exciting life you live, Delaney Reed."

"Maybe… maybe too exciting," I said quietly.

Instead of answering, his hand slid across the console to rest, warm and heavy, on my thigh.

"No. Exciting's good. What do we do with our possible suspect, Chief?"

"I say we just go ask him if he stole the lights. Flip has a bit of a language barrier with English, but he is honest and tends to interpret things literally. So we should get a straight answer out of him."

The wind shoveled rain across the parking lot. Huge, fat drops bounced off concrete like a million glass marbles.

We were going to have flooding for sure. The rivers couldn't take this much rain all at one go this late into the rainy season. I made a mental checklist to be sure we had eyes on the main highway and people ready to respond to downed trees, mud slides, and flooded roads.

"You think he'll tell you the truth?" Ryder asked.

I popped my hood up and latched the neck closure into place. "Let's find out."

Ryder had his hood up too. We got out and made quick work of intercepting Flip at his truck.

Bigfoot drove a beat-up Ford that blended right in with the cars in town. He'd parked under a tree where the streetlamp above threw more shadows than light. I scanned the open truck bed. Other than a toolbox bungeed down in the corner, it was empty.

Flip pushed the cart across the parking lot at speed, those long legs giving his lumbering gait a kind of grace one wouldn't expect from a cryptid his size.

Somehow his hat stayed jammed on his head despite the wind, but his trench coat was absolutely soaked by the time he reached us.

"Oh, hello," he said, his voice always a surprisingly soft singsong. As if he were more used to conversing with the sky or the wind or the small growing things below the trees than with people. With how reclusive he was, that was a pretty fair assessment.

"Hi, Flip," I said. "Let me introduce you to Ryder Bailey." I lined up my thoughts, wanting to get the order right for Flip: outward from the heart. "He is my love, my fiancé, a builder, and a reserve officer."

"Hi there, Ryder," Flip said.

"Nice to meet you," Ryder said. I could hear the excitement in his voice. For all that Ryder liked to play it cool about the magic and supernaturals in town, he was still new enough to it to be surprised and delighted when he met a new supernatural.

And let's face it, what person in the Pacific Northwest wouldn't want to meet the real Bigfoot?

Or at least one of them.

"This is business," I said, framing the conversation for Flip. My family had learned early on that details and, sometimes even subjects, got lost between Bigfoot's language and English.

"Business, is this?" he asked.

I nodded. "Someone stole a traffic light. Red, yellow, green." I held my hands so I could show him the approximate size of the thing. "Did you steal the traffic light?"

Flip frowned, which was a weird mashing of the spell-created human face, and his natural features which I could see beneath the spell.

"Steal the light, is that right?" he asked.

"That is right. Did you steal it?"

He shook his head slowly, then a little firmer. "Not I, no lie." He pressed his fingertips to his lips to further let me know he was telling the truth.

Then his eyes went big and watery. He turned his head just in time to heave a mighty sneeze, knocking his hat sideways.

"Okay, we don't want you to stay under that spell for any longer," I said. "I know you're allergic to it."

"Witches itches," he sputtered between two more huge sneezes.

"Just one quick thing," I said. "Someone took a light pole too. Did you steal a light pole?"

He shook his head, pressed fingers to his lips, his nostrils quivering, before he went off on another sneezing jag.

"Here," Ryder said. "Let's get your stuff in the truck."

We quickly helped him unload his cart into the cab. There was hot cocoa in there and marshmallows. A lot of marshmallows. Flip slid into the driver's side and pawed off the spell necklace, placing it carefully on the seat but as far away as he could.

Then he shook, a full body shiver from the ankles up to his head, and he was in his natural state. Bigfoot, in a busted-down old Ford truck, wearing a trench coat and a fedora.

Good thing he'd parked under the shadow of the tree.

Good thing a rainstorm was raging.

Good thing there weren't a lot of shoppers out.

Good thing I was standing close to Ryder, because I got to hear his little delighted gasp.

I smiled and mimed rolling down the window. Flip nodded and did so.

"If you see anyone taking the light structures in town, please let me know as soon as you can."

"I will, but still. It is our gathering we will be… havering…, having" He frowned again, and worked his mouth, thinking through the translations in his head.

I made a note to myself that I should really learn his language, but I just wasn't that good with whistles, purrs, and grunts.

"The moon is soon." He pointed at the roof of his truck, to where the moon might be if there weren't so many clouds in the sky. "I am off to our glen, where it will begin. The gathering we 'Foots will be... havering?" He frowned and tipped his head slightly.

"Having," I corrected. "So it's the gathering of all the families?"

"Exactly, Delaney." He smiled. "I am to speak to my heart." He pointed at Ryder. "We have been apart."

"You and your heart? You have a special person?" I asked. "Someone you love like I love Ryder?"

He grunted, and it was that mix of guttural and purr I had never been able to mimic. A sweetly goofy grin spread across his face. "My gifts will be bright, my song will be free, then my heart will come home with me."

"Here to Ordinary?" I asked. "That's wonderful, Flip. Remember to bring this heart person to me so I can meet them and explain the rules, okay?"

He grunted again, this one softer, higher.

"All right. So do tell me if you see anyone stealing lights," I reminded him. "And have a great time at the gathering."

He made a little hooting hum, and I knew that was a happy sound.

I stepped away from the truck; Ryder did the same, bringing the cart with him.

Flip rolled up the window, started the old truck, then rambled out of the parking lot, his indicator light flicking before he turned onto the road and headed north out of town.

"So what do you think?" I asked as we started back to the Jeep, Ryder stopping to swing the cart into the corral on the way past.

"I think I just met a real live Sasquatch. Who likes to rhyme."

"The rhyming thing is how English makes the most sense to him. But do you think he's telling the truth?"

"I wouldn't even know how to read his body language."

I glanced over at Ryder. Even in the rain, even in the dark and wind, his smile was bright.

"You liked him, didn't you?"

"I did."

"So you don't think he stole the traffic light?"

"He didn't look guilty to me. But you know him better. What do you think?"

We'd made it to the Jeep, and both got in as quickly as possible.

I started the engine to warm the vehicle but shivered anyway. Oregon storms hit to the bone even through layers of waterproofing and wool.

"I think I want dinner and a hot shower. And not necessarily in that order."

"I like the sound of that. Are you off the clock for the night, or do you have reports to file?"

I did have reports to file. Being a police officer meant the paperwork never ended. But the dash clock said it was 5:30. With the windstorm building, and a power transfer happening bright and early tomorrow morning, my best chance for food, downtime, and maybe even sleep was opting out of my habitual overtime.

"I am so done for the night," I said. "How about you? Any extra work waiting for you at the construction site?"

"Nope. That's buttoned down. Next project starts up in three weeks."

The reminder was there. Maybe he didn't mean it to be, but he would be slammed with business soon. Then we would be working the festivals, working our jobs, and dealing with everything else that happened in a town like ours. The window of time for our vacation—any one we picked—was swiftly closing.

This weekend was pretty much it.

I didn't bring it up again. Not while I was dripping wet and hungry.

"It appears we may have synchronized evenings off, Mr. Bailey," I teased instead.

"It appears we do. Any suggestions for how to fill our time, Ms. Reed?"

"Dinner?" I asked hopefully. "Shower?"

Ryder fiddled with the vents and held his hands over the one nearest him. "Someone might have left chicken marinating and fresh homemade bread cooling."

I groaned and my stomach rumbled at his words. "You are the best fiancé in the world."

He leaned toward me and gave me a quick, firm kiss. "That goes without saying. Now drive. I'm starving."

So I drove.

CHAPTER SEVEN

THE STORM WAS STILL RAGING, but Ryder had started the fire, and his dog, Spud, was over there snoring. The dragon pig was using the dog's butt for a pillow.

"New placemats?" I asked, tapping one of the half-dozen laminated mats on the kitchen island. It was a beautiful brochure touting all the fun things to do in Sedona. Next to that was Chicago, the Olympic rainforest, and a spelunking map.

Ryder straightened as he removed the food from the oven. "I had a little time on my hands."

I picked up Sedona, turned it over, and grinned when I saw a list written in Ryder's clean blocky script. "Pros: restaurants, artisans, wine tour, canyon tours, stars. Cons: too woo-woo."

"You think Sedona, Arizona, is too woo-woo? For the woman who spends her life dealing with gods and monsters and magic?"

"They have a buttload of energy vortexes there. Says so in the pamphlet."

"I think I can handle a few energy vortexes. At least they aren't gateways for demon spawn."

He turned with dinner: a pan of beautifully roasted chicken and vegetables with a sauce almost thick enough to be gravy. It smelled like heaven.

"That you know of."

"That we know of," I agreed.

"So you like the idea of Sedona, huh?" He settled dinner in the middle of the island, slightly to one side, then plucked serving utensils out of the drawer.

"I do like the idea of Sedona," I said.

He dished food, and I dished food. Once our plates were full, he asked, "But?"

I took a bit of chicken then a chunk of yam, both covered in garlic, rosemary and sage sauce. "Oh, my gods," I mumbled. "This is amazing."

"Thank you. I got the recipe from Myra. Back to Sedona. But?"

I sighed and put my fork down, twisting my fingers in the cloth napkin I'd dropped in my lap.

"I can't do it."

"Sedona?" He sat back, pulling his beer with him, but not taking a drink yet.

"Yeah. Too far. I mean if Death is going to be handling all the god powers while I'm gone, I think I need to stay relatively nearby."

He took a drink, waiting. The wind plowed over the roofing, tugging at the gutters and power lines.

"That makes sense. I'm not asking for the moon, Laney. I mean, unless we could book the moon."

I grinned. "Terrible restaurants on the moon."

"Oh?"

"No atmosphere at all."

He blinked. Blinked again. Then he gulped down half his beer and pointed it at me. "That was a terrible joke."

"No, it was perfect timing. For the *gravity* of our conversation. Get it? Gravity?"

He shoveled food in his mouth and just shook his head.

I followed his lead and ate dinner, enjoying every bite. I enjoyed the quiet, too, because I needed that sometimes. No questions, no demands, no conversation. Just our safe, comfy house around us. Just the two of us together.

"What about LaPine?" he finally asked. "The cabin. It's in a little forested area overlooking a glade. Hot tub on the deck. Out in the middle of almost nowhere. All the privacy we could want."

I sighed, picked up my beer and sipped. "Sounds like heaven. What days is it reserved for?"

"Tomorrow through Sunday."

"Four whole days?"

"Well, I could extend the stay. I just wasn't sure you would be willing to stay away any longer."

"Because of my job?"

He shrugged. "That. And this is our first time vacationing together. I thought we might want to try a few days and see how it went before we booked a month cruise somewhere."

"I am never going to cruise anywhere," I said. "I don't like boats nearly enough."

He grinned. "Good to know. I'm never spelunking."

"Good to know."

I stood and took our plates to the sink. "This is our only chance, isn't it?" I asked over the frothing of bubbles in the sink.

"To go on vacation?"

I nodded. He was twisted in his chair, watching me. I flicked bubbles his way and he batted them out of the air.

"We'll have other chances."

"But not for a long time," I said. "Maybe not until next year."

He finished his beer, then put both bottles in the recycle bin. "True. Plus, we have a wedding coming up. Lots to plan on top of everything else."

I groaned. "It's so much planning."

He chuckled and stepped up behind me, hands landing on my hips, then stroking down my jeans before he wrapped his arms around me, pressing his warmth and his strength against my body, his mouth near my ear. "I like planning extravagant things with you," he murmured, all sexy-like.

"A pizza tower isn't extravagant," I murmured back. "When I say fancy wedding, there better be some fancy stuff."

He exhaled and the warm burst of air on my neck made me shiver. Then he leaned in a little closer and bit gently at my earlobe. "But it's a whole tower. Made of pizza."

"I expect you to bring your A-game to these negotiations, Mr. Bailey."

He hummed and pressed a kiss to the base of my neck. Electricity ran through me: chest, spine, hips. Good thing I had already turned off the water or there'd have been bubbles all over the floor.

"How about a no-host bar?" he husked.

"Odin would kill me."

"We'll provide the fancy pretzels."

"Pretzels aren't fancy," I gasped, as his hands slipped around in front of me, fingers gently tugging my sweater up just enough for his hands to slip under and stroke my heated skin.

"We can make them fancy."

"How?"

"Chocolate-dipped pretzels."

"Still not fancy enough. And what about the cake?"

He tugged my earlobe a little harder. "Who needs a dumb cake? Just serve everyone chocolate pretzels. Easy. Cheap. Give them a can of whipped cream and let them go nuts." He deposited a hot, sucking kiss on my jaw.

I held my breath, so I didn't groan. As soon as his lips lifted, I spun to face him, my hand locked and loaded with a mountain of bubbles. "No cake?"

His eyes were huge as I smashed my palm into his face, bubbles flying in all directions.

He spit and sputtered. "You did not just shove soap in my mouth." He released me and backed up, bumping into the island.

"What's that?" I batted my eyes innocently. "You were telling me we're not going to have a *dumb* wedding cake? You want pretzels instead of a *dumb* wedding cake? I have been planning this wedding my whole life."

Not true. I'd been obsessed with eloping since I first heard about it. Mostly because eloping seemed like some kind of legal crime.

"There had better be all sorts of fancy things happening at our wedding. Including cake."

His eyes narrowed, and he tipped his head down. But that smile was all sin. "I think you better run, Delaney Reed. Or I won't be held accountable for my actions."

I stood there, vibrating, knowing this was a game and the chase was on.

But instead of running, instead of making him chase me, I walked to him slowly, stood so close I could see his heartbeat through his shirt, could feel his need in waves radiating off him.

"I like the sound of action," I said. "No accountability required." Then I kissed him until the world faded and only we remained.

CHAPTER EIGHT

Two things happened at once: the knocking on the front door turned into pounding, and a brick wall fell on top of me.

"Ow," I muttered, pushing at the brick wall. "Get off, bud."

The brick wall grunted, then growled a very dragon-y growl. A soft piggy nose snuffled my palm, hot dragon breath washing over my skin.

I opened my eyes.

Dragon pig sat on my thighs, weighing roughly as much as a firehouse, wagging its tiny pink tail.

It *oink*ed once, and that *oink* sounded very satisfied. It also smelled weirdly electric.

The pounding at the front door stopped, then started up again. This time just a knuckle rapping out the beat to a song. Sounded like the base line to "We Will Rock You."

"Is that Queen?" Ryder's voice was muffled by the

pillow covering his head. Spud sat like a good boy on the floor but was big enough he could lick Ryder's ears if Ryder didn't take morning pillow position.

I pushed up on my elbows, pointed at the dragon pig. "Off please. I'll get you breakfast after I deal with the door."

"Thank you," Ryder mumbled. "Coffee too?"

I leaned over and kissed my man on the bare shoulder, right by his tattoo. "I was talking to the dragon pig."

Then I yanked the pillow off his head. He scrabbled for it.

"Too slow," I grinned. I smacked him in the face.

He howled. I ran out of the bedroom as he hollered threats I knew he'd never actually follow through on.

I got to the door before he'd even launched out of bed, and when he skidded into the living room, I held up a warning finger. "Someone's at the door."

He was wearing boxer briefs and nothing else, his hair sticking up on one side. He crossed those gorgeous arms over his hard chest and leaned his shoulder against the wall.

"Go ahead," he said. "I'll wait."

I tucked my hair behind my ears and made sure Ryder's T-shirt, which I'd thrown on last night, covered my underwear.

Good enough.

I looked through the peephole and groaned.

Crow waggled his fingers at me and kept knocking.

I threw the chains and locks and opened the door. "What?" I asked. "I haven't had coffee yet. You should know I have killed men for trying to talk to me before I am caffeinated."

"Bunny-boo," Crow said. "This is your Uncle Crow. You know I'll take care of you." He lifted his other hand which held a coffee carrier and three large, lidded cups of coffee.

I tore my gaze away from the delicious smelling beverage and studied him.

"What do you want?"

He smiled like a lying Mc-lying-faced liar. "Coffee with my favorite Reed sister." He lifted the cups higher.

He was so full of shit. I knew this was a bad idea, but I hadn't had coffee yet, and I tended to make the worst decisions before breakfast.

"Okay, fine." I stepped out of the way so he could come inside. "But I know you're here for something."

"I am," he agreed, unzipping his hoodie. "I'm here for coffee. But look at you, Ryder Bailey. That six pack is making me jealous. Also a little turned on, if I'm honest."

Ryder rolled his eyes and turned toward the bedroom. "Delaney, you want me to bring your pants?"

"Yes."

Crow watched Ryder walk away, then pivoted on the balls of his feet. "Wow," he whispered. "Didn't he grow up nice?"

I grabbed the carrier out of his hands and stomped off to the kitchen. "You've seen him in his swim trunks every summer. All that isn't anything you haven't seen before." I pulled one of the cups out of the cardboard and took a huge swallow.

Hot, bitter, with chocolate and caramel to take the sting out of it. Delicious. "That's my fiancé you're ogling, Crow."

"And can I just say how happy I am for you two kids. Starting a new life together, soulmates finally tying the knot. Like some kind of dream come true."

I narrowed my eyes and gulped down half the cup. The caffeine hadn't hit yet, but the heat of the drink, and the shifty-eyed god who'd brought it had woken me up. All the way awake.

So awake, I knew what this visit was about. Well, not the details, but the basics for sure.

"What did you do?" I asked.

Crow strolled over, his hands behind his back. His forest-green hoodie was wet at the shoulders but not soaked all the way through. The storm had finally blown itself out in the early hours of the morning leaving a cloudy sky and only spits of rain.

"I brought you coffee," he said, taking one of the seats at the kitchen island.

"Uh-huh. And?"

"And Ryder too. And one for me. So we can all have a nice cup of coffee together."

"Why?"

Ryder came through the kitchen with Spud and the dragon pig hot on his heels.

Ryder had changed into jeans and a white Henley shirt under a navy flannel. He came straight to me, kissed me on the mouth, then pressed my favorite pair of jeans into my hands.

90

"Morning," he murmured.

I smiled, liking him this close. Liking that freckle on the edge of his eyebrow, the laugh lines at his eyes, the smell of his deodorant mixed with the caramel scent of coffee.

"Morning."

"Morning, Ryder," Crow cooed.

"What did you do?" Ryder asked, moving to the door.

Crow made an affronted sound. "I have no idea what you're talking about."

Ryder opened the door so Spud and the dragon pig could go outside and do their business. Not that the dragon pig actually did any business, but it liked to trot around in the yard so the other creatures understood that this yard, this house, and those within it were its domain.

"You brought us coffee." I shoved my legs into my jeans. "It's five in the morning. I know all the steps to your little dance of unaccountability, so whatever you're about to tell me is absolutely your fault, and you're going to have to clean up your mess. Talk."

Crow reached over, plucked up a cup and took a sip. "You were such a quiet child. How did you grow up so…"

I raised an eyebrow.

He laughed. "All right, fine. This wasn't my fault."

Ryder snorted and took the last cup in the holder.

I made the hurry-up signal, rolling my finger. "Get to the point."

"Well, there's good and bad news."

"Talk, or I'll tell Bertie you're going to be her new right-hand man for anything she needs to keep the festivals running."

"Yowza. You're leading with the big guns this morning, aren't you?" he asked.

"Talk, Crow."

He took another deep swallow of coffee, held up his finger, then put the coffee on the counter and stepped back.

That was not a good sign.

"So, good news, the storm broke." He smiled. "Bad news, some of the roads are flooded and a driftwood log slammed into The Whistling Sails, busting out a wall, some windows, and knocking down the balcony."

"Shit." I jogged to the bedroom for my phone.

"No one was hurt," he called after me. "The motel rooms weren't rented out. So that's good news too, isn't it? See how I'm a bringer of good news?"

I pushed the comforter, which had fallen off the bed, to one side. "Where's my phone?" I said. "Ryder?"

He was there, on the other side of the bed, checking in the sheets. "Nightstand?

"No."

"Dresser?"

"No."

He dropped to his knees and reached under the bed. "Got it. Oh."

"Oh?"

Ryder stood. "I'm gonna blame the dragon pig." He held the phone out to me. Or rather he held half the phone out to me, the bottom half having been neatly bitten off.

"It ate my phone?" I took the destroyed electronic, having to actually touch the broken and melted edges to believe it. "It ate *half* my phone. Why? Why would it do this?"

"Did you feed it yesterday?"

"It had some forks and lug nuts at the diner."

"That's barely a snack for that thing. I thought you were getting some old guard rails for it to eat."

"Fencing. Metal fencing." And because it was morning and because I had been distracted by Crow, it all fell into place. I groaned. "Which I forgot to pick up from Aaron."

Ryder cleared his throat. It sounded like he was covering a laugh.

I glanced up at him. "Don't." I scowled.

He curved his fingers over his mouth and chin.

"I can still see you grinning like a maniac. This isn't funny."

"Totally not funny." He sounded like he was going to bust a lung trying to keep the laugh at bay.

"I don't have a backup phone," I whined. "How am I going to check in on The Whistling Sails?"

"You could get a new one. If the road to Salem isn't flooded."

"It is," Crow called from the living room. "Part of 101 slid off the hill. Crews are working on it, but it's gonna take more than a day to get it stabilized."

I dropped the half phone into the trash can. "So either I have to drive the long way south through

Newport, hoping the pass is clear, or go without a phone."

"And did I mention the other bad news?" Crow called out.

"Is it wrong of me to want to strangle my almost-uncle?" I whispered.

"I don't know," Ryder whispered back. "Have you tried it?"

I grinned at him. He grinned back and called, "Spill it, Crow. What's the bad news?"

I shucked out of Ryder's T-shirt and threw on a sweater, then dug out a pair of socks. Phone or no phone, I was going to be outside today checking in with everyone and assessing the storm damage. Another storm was scheduled to hit later tonight. We weren't out of the woods yet.

I grabbed a rubber band and finger-combed my hair back to get it out of my way. Ryder was ahead of me, letting the dog and dragon pig back inside.

"Bad dragon," Ryder said as the pink menace trotted in a cute little circle around his feet. "But you're probably starving. Thank you for not eating my truck."

It sat on its soft butt and tipped its snout up. It *oink*ed once, adorably.

Ryder headed toward the garage. "How about a crappy set of golf clubs for breakfast?" He got another *oink* for an answer and the dragon pig galloped after him.

"Could I interest you in an incredibly annoying pet?" I asked Crow.

"Why, what'd it do?"

"Ate my phone," I grumbled. "Okay, tell me the rest of it. All of it." I snagged up my boots from where I'd left them in the front entryway.

"Electricity's out," Crow said.

"Where?"

"Just the shoreline and the bay. Some places are working on backup generators." He held up the hot coffee as proof.

"You know, it's weird you're the one telling me all this. Where are my sisters?"

"I ran into them and offered to come by."

"Suspicious." I balanced on one foot, shoved the other in my boot, and repeated the process.

"You really gotta try looking on the bright side one of these days, Boo Boo." Crow took another swig of coffee.

"What's the bright side?"

"Me," he said, like it was obvious. "I'm the brightest bright you've ever seen. Oh, and also I think we have a little time before all hell breaks out."

Ryder had lugged the golf clubs into the living room, leaving the pig to its feast. He handed me my coat. I just held it in my fist, wanting nothing more than to throw it at Crow's head. Then maybe strangle him with it.

"You make me crazy," I said. "If you're not going to tell me, I'll just go ask Myra. Or Jean. Have fun being Bertie's lackey for the next decade."

I angled into my coat, reached for the door.

"Wait!"

I didn't release the door but threw him a look over my shoulder.

The smile was gone. The teasing was gone. He'd set his coffee cup on the kitchen island, and now he shoved both his hands, stiff-fingered, into the front pockets of his jeans.

"I just found out. I need you to remember that, because I know you, Delaney, and I know you are going to lose your mind. But I just found out. This morning. And that is the full truth."

I turned the handle.

"All right. Hold it. I know." He licked his lips, shrugged one shoulder up like his neck was cramping, then mumbled: "I know who the storage unit belonged to."

"What?" I asked. "Louder. I don't have ears on the floor."

He lifted his gaze to mine. "The storage unit. You asked me where I got most of that stuff?"

"The whale sale?"

"Yeah."

"Storage units, right?"

He nodded. "Three, but most of it, the good stuff, the stuff that really sold well, was from one unit."

"Whose unit?"

"Pandora's."

This time I did let go of the handle so I could smash my hand over my face. It was better than grabbing my uncle and shaking the feathers out of him.

"Uh, Delaney. Boo Boo. Did you hear me?"

I inhaled, exhaled, counted down from ten, no, twenty, no, one hundred.

"All that stuff I sold used to be owned by Pandora."

Ninety…

"Which pretty much makes her storage unit a box, doesn't it?" he mused.

Eighty…

"Most of the stuff came in a box, too, now that I think of it."

Seventy…

"So that's gonna be a problem if the myths are to be believed."

"Of course the myths are to be believed!" I waved my hands around. "This is Ordinary."

"I know where we live, Delaney," he said. "Which is why as soon as I found out who the items used to belong to, I insisted I would come over here and fill you in. See? I'm doing my part to keep everyone safe."

I just stared at him, and the stupid twinkle in his eye that said he rather liked the way things were turning out so far.

Trickster gods were just the worse, but Crow was the worst of them all.

"So is the weather and flooding and destruction of property because Pandora's stuff was sold?" Ryder asked.

It was good he'd said something. What I needed right now was focus and a clear head. And Crow just looked so strangle-able.

"I don't think so," I said, turning away from Crow even

though all I wanted to do was stay here and yell. Yelling wouldn't solve the problem, and I was pretty sure Crow was right when he said all hell was going to break loose.

"So what's the hell that's going to break loose?" Ryder opened the door for me, his brain putting two and two together and coming up with the next logical step at the same time as mine.

"I don't know yet," I said. "But if all the items came in boxes…"

"…and the storage unit is a box," he added.

"…then everything Crow sold has the potential of being cursed."

Ryder jogged with me to the Jeep and waited for me to unlock it so he could get in the passenger seat. Unfortunately, Crow was right behind us.

"Hey, don't look at me like that," he said. "You told me this was my mess to clean up, so I'm coming with you to clean it up."

I leaned on the top of the driver's door and glared at him over the roof of the vehicle. "I want a list of everything you got out of the storage unit, *and* a list of everyone who bought something from you."

"You think I keep track of all the—"

"Yes," I interrupted. "I know you do. Get the lists. Then call me."

"Phone," Ryder said.

"Shit. Call Ryder, he'll be with me. If we're going to find all this stuff before curses start popping up everywhere, we're going to have to split up and be quick."

"But…"

"No. Go. Get the records. Call. Now."

I ducked into the Jeep.

Ryder was already on his phone texting.

"Who?" I asked.

"Myra." He hit the screen, and Myra's voice came through the speaker.

"Crow did what?"

"Sold Pandora's box. Boxes," I clarified.

"Want me to try to get the manifest of what was in her storage?"

"No, I have Crow doing that. I need you to head to the library and see if there's any way we can tell which of the items she owned are cursed."

"Is there a chance none of them are?" Ryder asked.

"No," Myra and I said at the same time.

"Once you get to the library, let me know," I said.

"Already there," she said.

Relief washed through me. Myra. Right place, right time. "Okay, then let me know what you find out. If all of this stuff is cursed, we're going to need a curse breaker."

"Got it." She sounded a little out of breath like she was climbing stairs.

"I'm sending Jean south. We'll need to coordinate if we're repossessing or curse-breaking the objects."

"Curse-breaking is best," she said. "That way we won't have to deal with this same problem in ten years when the items crop up again."

"Agreed. I'll check in with Hatter and Shoe, make sure they're dealing with the weather-related disasters."

"Good," Myra said. "Delaney?"

"Yeah?"

"You promised me you were going on vacation today."

I looked at Ryder, and he was staring straight ahead. He felt my gaze, though, and looked down at the phone.

"Reservations are good for a late check in," he said.

"Wouldn't have to be a late check in if you left right now," Myra said.

Ryder's eyes came up, and I was caught by the green of them, flecked with black and gold, like a forest in the setting sun. There was a question in his eyes, an invitation. We could just run away. Leave this mess behind.

I could just let go.

He must have seen something in my expression because to Myra he said, "We're good for now. Headed north." He paused.

I nodded. "Yeah, north."

"And we'll work our way down as soon as Crow gets us the list of buyers." He raised his eyebrow in question, and I nodded. That was the plan. He knew me well.

"If you need me," I said, "call Ryder's phone."

"Why? What's wrong with your phone?"

"It got eaten by a dragon."

She laughed and kept on laughing until Ryder pressed the button to hang up on her.

I eased the Jeep out onto the street and took off northward. Limbs had fallen in yards, on roofs, and cars, but no major damage that I could see. A couple of fences were blown over and garbage cans rearranged.

Winter on the Oregon coast meant we were prepared for these kinds of storms. We'd taken a lot worse damage, so I knew we would get through this. But with another storm coming in tonight, it was best to do everything we could before it hit.

Like find all the cursed objects before something terrible happened.

"So on a scale of time-to-go-on-vacation to oh-my-gods-we're-gonna-die, where do the cursed items fall?" he asked.

"Probably varies. If we have Pandora's past to measure against, I'd say we're somewhere in dump-truck-of-shit-about-to-hit-jet-engine territory."

"Well, crap," he said.

"Exactly." I aimed the Jeep north, noting with relief that the main drag through town was relatively clear from debris. The missing traffic light wasn't helping anything, but we were used to having power knocked out several times a year too. We'd set up road construction sawhorses with flashing lights to warn everyone to use the intersection like a four-way stop.

So far, no accidents. Luckily, this wasn't the busy tourist season.

Ryder's phone belted out the opening to "Drop it Low, Girl" by Ester Dean. I gave him a wide-eyed look.

He just flashed me a grin, mouthed, "*drop it drop it low,*" before hitting the screen. "You're on speaker, Crow. I'm with Delaney. What you got?"

"The list of names and items. I think there's only a couple dozen things from Pandora's stash."

"Forward it to Ryder," I said, "we'll take it from here."

"Now, now," Crow said. "I seem to recall someone

telling me that if I made the mess, I needed to be the one to clean it up."

"No," I said.

"So, I'll meet you wherever you're headed."

"No—Shit. Did you see that?"

Ryder nodded. "Kind of hard to miss a giant yellow flash. Power lines?"

"That's what we'll say it was," I said.

"Blue Owl?" Ryder asked.

"Looks like it."

"Piper bought one," Crow said. "I'll meet you there."

"Crow, you will do no such thing."

Ryder shook his head and held up his phone. "He hung up." His phone chimed. "That's the list."

"Forward it to everyone."

"Already ahead of you."

"What did Piper buy?" I stepped on the gas, the standing water throwing up wings as I plowed through deep puddles.

"Hang on." He worked his phone, fielding messages and scanning through the list.

"Well," he grumbled, "one thing I can say about Crow. He keeps detailed records."

"Such as?"

"*Piper: good mood, French perfume, no jewelry, paid cash.*"

"All right. Paid cash for what?"

"A toy."

"Does he say what kind?"

Ryder scowled at the screen. "*Solar dancing toy. Clapper.* I have no idea what that is."

I bit my bottom lip. "Does it say outside or inside toy?"

"No."

"That's fine," I said. "We can ask Piper. I'm sure she knows what she bought."

He nodded. "Plus, Crow's meeting us there."

"Yeah, I'd rather keep him out of this as much as possible."

"You did tell him to clean up his messes."

"And yet he always finds some way to mess up his messes even more."

"Talented."

"Trickster."

"You sure you don't want to get away? Little cabin in the woods. Might be snowy. Hot tub. Peaceful. Quiet. Just the two of us. Heaven."

He was teasing me a little, but I needed him to know exactly how I felt. "I want that more than anything. The faster we take out Pandora's trash, the faster we get that hot tub. And it better be peaceful and quiet. Just the two of us."

"I love it when you get all forceful." He patted his chest and fluttered his eyes.

I pulled into the diner's parking lot, avoiding the ruts and puddles. "All right, let's go see what that flash was all about."

The wind had picked up, cold and wet off the ocean. It wasn't raining, but the air still had tiny droplets in it, forming a mist that was almost invisible. It was the kind of moisture that wasn't really noticeable until you'd been standing in it for several minutes and realized you were soaking wet.

Typical Oregon.

"I'll take point." I strode up to the door.

He nodded and fell into step behind me.

The diner looked normal. Half-a-dozen cars were parked as close to the building as possible so the owners wouldn't have to walk far through the rain. The smell of cinnamon and onions—weirdly, a nice mix—poured out of the venting.

From what I could see through the windows, diners were at tables eating breakfast. There must be some really great music playing on the janky speakers because every head in the place was nodding along to the beat.

Which was...

"Weird," Ryder said. "The synchronized head-bopping. That's weird, right?"

"That's weird."

I pushed through the door and stopped.

"Hey, Delaney," Piper said. She was plastered against the wall next to me, her eyes wide and staring straight out over the dining area. "Thought you'd be by. Wanna fill me in on what's going on?"

I didn't tell her I was just about to ask the same thing.

"Did you buy a toy from Crow?" I asked.

"Toy?"

"Solar-powered clapper?" Ryder hadn't stepped into the building at all, but stood in the threshold of the door, letting in the wet, fresh air.

"Yeah," she said. "I did."

"Is it here?"

She still hadn't taken her eyes off the far side of the diner. As a matter of fact, other than talking, she hadn't moved at all.

"Can't you see it?" she asked.

I scanned the room. Three booths and two tables were occupied. Every person was sitting still, hands in front of them, heads bobbing side to side. Side to side.

The music was a slow country tune, and the beat of the song and the beat of the diners was not lining up at all.

But it wasn't just the bobbing heads that were a problem. Everyone in my line of vision had blank stares on their faces. It was like they were listening to a hypnotist put them under a thrall from far away.

"What are they doing?" Ryder asked. "All the people?"

I didn't know, but luckily, someone did. "You can't hear it?" Piper asked. "The voice?"

"No," Ryder and I said at the same time.

"As soon as I unboxed the little guy and stuck him in the window, it started talking. At first, I thought it was just static on the radio or something. But then I remembered we stream our own playlists."

"That's very modern of you," I said.

"Thank you. I just had it installed after Christmas. People really seem to like it."

"So what is the voice saying?" Ryder asked.

"Sad things. So many sad things."

That's when I noticed the tears. No one was wailing or sobbing. But all these people were sitting here, bopping their heads, silently crying. That made the whole thing worse.

"Okay, I'm creeped out. Where's the clapper?"

Piper tried to lift her hand, but grimaced. "If I move, I'm not going to be able to tune out the voice. Window," she said. "Window."

Great. The entire place was made of windows. I focused on the sills and noted there were dozens and dozens of little plastic figures, waving and wobbling. Flowers, cats, horses, people set on stands with little solar panels at the bottom, all of them rocking and swinging.

These little toys had been popular several years ago, and yes, they were cute. But too many cute things all collected together was how people got eaten in horror movies.

I took a careful step forward. Ryder's hand landed on my arm. "I don't like you going in there alone. I can hear it now. Can't you hear the voice?"

I turned. My man was pale, his eyes wide. Tears tracked down his face. I could tell he was torn about staying behind or going forward with me.

Ryder was human. He had been claimed by a god and that had changed him in some ways, but mostly, he was human.

Because I came from a family line blessed by all the deities who had made this town, I was a lot more tolerant of magic. It wasn't that I was unaffected by magic, but usually it didn't hit me as hard as it hit other mortals.

"It's okay," I said. "You stay here."

"But." He sucked in a shaky breath, and the tears poured harder, making his eyes red. "How are you going to stop it?"

"Box," Piper said. "Counter."

If the demigod was struggling to keep the voice at bay, I knew the time I had to find the cursed clapper and stuff it back into the box— if I could find the box—was short.

"Well, isn't this great?" Crow strolled up behind Ryder. "Move aside, Bailey."

"Can't," Ryder sniffed.

"It's some kind of sadness spell," I said. "They hear a voice."

Crow cocked his head, the feather in his ear flipping in the wind.

"Okay, yeah. I can hear it. Distantly. Where's the little monkey?"

"It's a monkey? Okay, I'll find it," I told him. "You find the box behind the counter."

Crow ducked under Ryder's arm and squeezed past him through the door.

I strode into the room, missing Ryder's hand on my arm as soon as I was out of reach.

The music had switched to something upbeat and cute about wearing colors for someone's return, but the song sounded strange.

Like there was another song playing.

Or like there was another voice singing right over the top of the melody line.

Great. I could hear the little bastard's voice. But that

wasn't the worst of it. The worst of it was the words were in a language I had never heard before.

And everything about those words—the tone, the rhythm, the delivery—was undeniably, crushingly sad.

This was nothing like hearing god powers. The sound of the curse was like fingernails scrabbling down the inside of my brain.

I wanted to hide. I wanted to turn around and run. Because I knew all the sorrow I'd experienced in my life was a deep, deep well I did not want to fall to the bottom of.

I held on to all the other sounds in the place: the upbeat song, the wind against the windows, the *click, click, click*ing of the toys, and Crow's off-tune whistling as he rummaged through the storage shelves behind the counter.

Sad, sad, sad.

I pushed the feeling as far away as I could and drilled my way through the unnaturally thick air toward the first window.

So many little plastic smiling things. Cat in a swing, chick in an egg, and the monkey! Could it really be that easy? The first window I searched had the one cursed toy I needed to find?

I snatched the toy off the windowsill. Disappointment pressed hard on my sternum, mixing with the sadness I was barely keeping at bay. It wasn't a monkey, it was the Pope.

Dammit.

I replaced the Pope with a mumbled apology, then

moved to the next window. Flower, flower, snail, alien, double flower, camel on a toilet, bear.

No monkey.

The farther I pressed into the diner, the louder the voice became. I was losing track of the peppy color song, losing track of the sound of semi-trucks driving across wet road, losing track of the sound of my own voice in my head, naming each *clicky-clacky* plastic wavy-wacky thing.

I didn't know why I hadn't noticed all of them when I was in here yesterday. I didn't know why that *clack clack clack*ing hadn't driven me out of my mind.

Probably because there hadn't been a Pandora level curse in action when I'd last been here.

But the one thing I could hear above all the *sad, sad, sad* was Crow's stupid whistling. I thought he might be trying to do the song from the Robin Hood cartoon, but I couldn't be sure. Whatever he was trying to whistle, I was pretty sure he owed Roger Miller an apology.

The next window was tricky because a young couple sat in front of it. I didn't recognize them, so they were probably just traveling through.

"Sorry," I said, as I leaned over the ham-and-cheese omelets they were ignoring. I was all but invisible to them as I studied the click-clackers.

Scarecrow, flower, witch, farm girl. Okay, I could see this windowsill was themed. Apple tree, tin man, lion, dog.

No monkey, flying or not.

"Got it!" Crow called out.

I glanced over my shoulder. Crow was grinning

behind the counter, a red-and-gold-embossed cardboard box in his hand. "Find it yet?"

I shook my head because words felt a little unstable with every other thought in my head dripping, *sad, sad, sad*.

"Hurry up, Boo Boo," Crow said. "I think we're losing them."

To my horror, an old guy at the far booth slumped forward, his beard landing in a pillow of biscuits and gravy.

"No!" I rushed to the far end of the diner. I didn't know what I could do to stop this, but no one was going to die in their breakfast on my watch.

The voice grew louder, the clacking clacked louder. I made it to the man's side and reached for my phone to call an ambulance.

I patted my pocket over and over before I remembered my phone was toast.

"Dammit." I checked for the man's pulse. He was alive, his pulse strong and even.

Not dead. Just knocked out.

"Delaney?" Crow asked from what seemed like a world away, his voice somewhere out there on a distant horizon, all but smothered by another voice.

Sad, sad, sad.

It was so loud, so in my head, it was like it was right next to me, screaming in my ear.

I glanced up at the windowsill. Sunshine, cloud, rainbow, and finally, *finally*, monkey.

It was a creepy little thing. It was meant to resemble a baby chimp, but its face was too yellow, its eyes too red. It sat hunched up with two big cymbals in its hands, clapping them together to the head-bopping beat.

Okay, I got it. Clapper.

But what really made the little monkey creepy was that voice. It was not happy at all. Wave after wave of sadness and sorrow radiated off the little fuzz ball of grief as it *clack*ed and *clack*ed with the never-ending power of the sun.

If you're sad and you know it, clack, clack, clack…

"Gotcha." I tugged it off of the shelf in such a hurry, I tipped over the rainbow and didn't pause to right it.

Holy hells, the grief was even more concentrated now that I was holding the thing.

I knew I had to walk back across the diner. Knew I had to get the monkey to Crow so we could shove it in the box. So we could find some way to contain the curse.

But every breath was heavy. The room was going darker and darker. And I was cold.

Cold and alone.

If you're sad and you know it, then you really gotta show it…

No, I wasn't alone. I had Ryder with me. I had my sisters. I had this town and all these people and deities and others who made up my big, wild, vibrant family.

Plus, I had that Reed stubbornness.

I set my shoulders and turned back toward the front of the diner. Every step was like walking through deep water in the middle of a storm. Every thought was blanked out by the yelling, howling, cursing grief.

Why would anyone even want to put this kind of sorrow out into the world?

I tipped my head down and bulled forward, sweat prickling between my shoulders, under my arms, edging my hairline.

Fighting sadness was damn hard work.

I thought I'd made it at least halfway across the floor, but when I blinked away sweat to check my progress, I'd only made it about three feet.

Maybe I should rip off the monkey's head. Would that make it stop sadding all over the place? Knowing my luck, it would increase the potency of the curse.

The three people at the table ahead of me slumped down into their breakfasts. I winced because the woman had face-planted into a stack of pancakes with black-berry jam. The white headband she was wearing was ruined.

I could do this. I *had* to do this before the sorrow spread.

"Hey, all right, just." Crow was suddenly there, shining like a silver lining around the clouds in my head, his hands sure and strong as he turned the monkey in my hand.

"It should be... Where is the...?" He let go of the monkey.

Trying to support it was like holding a brick, except that the brick was made of lead and my arms were made of mashed potatoes.

"Maybe it's in... Ah-ha! There we are."

My sweaty grip was slipping. I didn't want to let the monkey fall, didn't want to break it in case the shattered

SEALED WITH A TRYST

monkey bits would spread the curse even more. But there was no way I could hold on to the slippery little jerk much longer.

Crow finally plucked the toy out of my hands. He pressed a butterfly sticker with one wrinkled wing on the monkey's butt and dropped the toy into the box. A glob of glowing gold radiated around the monkey for a moment, then Crow pushed the lid down so fast, it farted.

"There," he said. "That should do it."

The light returned to the world, the sky outside brightening, the crackly old speakers humming to life with a mellow, bluesy folk song.

I blinked a couple times and took a deep breath, my pulse falling back into a lighter rhythm. It felt like someone had just untwisted a phantom vice from around my heart.

"Are you all right there, Boo Boo?" Crow bent to catch my gaze.

I felt like a wrung-out mop, my muscles noodles, like I'd really gone overboard in the gym for a week straight.

"That sucked," I said.

"Little guy carried a kick." Crow frowned. "Are you sure you're okay?"

I wiped my arm over my forehead to wick away the sweat. "Peachy."

Everyone else in the room was rousing too. The people who'd fallen asleep on their plates wiped a mix of confusion and breakfast foods off their faces with napkins, looking around like they'd just woken from a quick, refreshing nap.

Piper, a force of energy, was already moving, working her way between the tables with quick efficiency. She seemed to know just what everyone needed whether it was fresh coffee, orange juice, or nice warm, damp towels for cleaning up faces and hands. She assured the sleepers replacement meals were already underway, and conversations rose up again, people chuckling, and chatting.

As if nothing had happened.

As if they hadn't all been cursed with so much sorrow it had almost sent them into comas.

As if magic had never been here.

Ordinary, the land blessed by hundreds of gods, the air fresh with life and mingled with the power of hundreds of supernatural creatures and people, had a way of sort of smoothing over minor magical moments.

I counted my lucky stars that the unusual nature of this event was whisked away and made to feel like something to chuckle about in the space of just a few moments. Something to maybe tell friends, but nothing to truly frighten or cause undo suspicion.

"Let's get that to the station where we can lock it away until we figure out how to break the curse."

"Look who put on her voice of authority one leg at a time today," Crow said. "I like it. Does this mean you're going to deputize me?"

"Not on your life." I started across the room, moving easier now, breathing easier as time erased the roughest edges of the experience.

Crow laughed, and that made something else lift in me. We'd survived our first curse. I was proud of us.

"You good?" Ryder asked, as I stepped after him out into the cool, wet air.

"Cabin in the mountain, right?" I asked.

"That's the plan."

"Hot tub. Just us. Solitude?"

"Yep."

"Let's get this done and get the hell outta town."

Ryder's smiled and, yeah, I smiled in return.

CHAPTER NINE

"You know what doesn't make sense?" I paused at the makeshift four-way stop, Ryder in the passenger seat.

"That Pandora left all this stuff behind in the first place and never told anyone the things were all cursed bombs waiting to go off?" he said.

"Well, that. But what set off the curse in the first place?"

"Opening the box?" he suggested.

"Naw," Crow said from the back seat. He had insisted he needed to ride with us because I'd told him it was his job to clean up the mess. I thought he was enjoying the whole thing.

"If unboxing triggered the curse," Crow went on, "my whale sale would have been a hell of a lot more fun."

I scowled at him in the rearview mirror. "Nothing weird happened at the sale?"

"Other than Ginny and Misty yelling about their crotches? Nothing."

"I don't believe you on principle."

"My heart," Crow said, tapping his chest. "Be still it."

"Maybe something about the storm triggered it?" Ryder said, ignoring Crow.

I shook my head. "I don't think so. Weather isn't used as a magical trigger very often. Too unpredictable."

He grunted.

"I think it has something to do with Bigfoot," Crow said.

"Why would it have something to do with him?" I asked.

"He stopped at my sale on his way out of town."

"I didn't see him there."

"He came in after you."

"Did he buy anything?"

"No, but he walked out with his pockets full."

"He stole stuff?" Ryder asked.

"He took some things, yeah."

"And you let him?" Ryder asked.

Crow shrugged. "I buy this stuff in lots. I don't expect to make money on all of it. Better someone get use out of it than I pay to take it to the dump."

"Do you know what he took?" I asked.

"Me? I'm not one of the all-knowing gods, Delaney."

"Crow."

He grinned. "Of course I know what he took. You know I keep track. Why did you even ask?"

"Because unlike some people in this vehicle, I follow the rules."

He chuckled. "Like taking your yearly vacations?"

"I follow all the rules," I said. "The vacation thing is more of a policy."

"Is that why you get grumpy and yell at Myra and Jean to take their days off?"

I scowled at him. He didn't look the least bit concerned, sprawled out in the seat, his arm thrown across the back, one ankle propped on his knee. He looked like he was having the trickster time of his trickster life.

"What did Flip take that has anything to do with Pandora's garage sale?" I asked.

"Some electric wire. I think. I mean, I'm not sure it was stuff from Pandora's unit. It's a lot to keep track of."

I slammed on the brakes. I wasn't going that fast, so Ryder easily braced, but Crow wasn't expecting the abrupt stop. He jerked forward, hands slamming into the seat back to keep him from knocking his head on it.

"Rude," he said.

"Here's what you're going to tell me," I said with a calm I thought even Myra would be impressed with. "Do you know what is setting off the cursed items?"

"I have a theory."

"Tell me."

"The butterfly."

"Butterfly?"

"The sticker? Little butterfly sticker I very carefully replaced on the monkey toy?"

"The one you took forever to dig out of the box?"

"It took me what? A minute? Two tops. Don't give

me that face. Now that I think about it, everything that came out of her storage unit had a butterfly sticker on it. Weird."

"Not weird," Ryder said. "Hope. It means hope. The butterfly."

"I think you're right. Hope was the last thing in Pandora's box," I said. "It fits the myth. When people remove the butterfly—when they give up hope—the curse kicks in."

Crow pointed a finger at me. "Smart."

"Okay, we can work with this. Ryder, let everyone know the butterfly stickers will shut the curse down."

"On it." He texted, his fingers fast over the screen of his phone.

I liked the look on his face—well, honestly, I liked all the looks on his face. But this one, engaged, concentrating, serious, was just so sexy that I wanted to reach over and put my hands all over him.

"Watch the road," he said without looking up.

"I am— Oh."

Crow chuckled as I swerved away from the shoulder. "I was avoiding a puddle," I said to my almost-uncle.

He just held up both hands, a grin on his face.

"I let them know we got the monkey," Ryder said, finishing something on his phone. "Told them about the sticker."

"Good, so we just need to—"

A blast of yellow light lanced into the stormy sky, looking like a lightning bolt striking upward, swallowed by the clouds.

"Crap," I said. "The lake?"

"Yes, cut here." Ryder pointed.

I threw on the Jeep's lights, red and blue strobing, as I broke the speed limit to get to the lake.

"Check on Jean…"

"She's not answering. But her location is three streets south."

I swung the Jeep south and floored it.

"There."

I followed Ryder's finger to Jean's parked truck, Myra's cruiser right next to it. The little cottage-style house had weathered, cedar-shake siding and a detached garage. A garage that was smoking.

"Call the fire department." I ran out of the Jeep, knowing Ryder was already on it.

Running into a burning building was a terrible idea, but if anyone was in there, if my sisters were in there, there was no way in hell I wasn't going to save them.

Three steps before I reached the door, it burst open as if it had been kicked.

My sisters appeared out of a billowing cloud of smoke, four teenagers behind them.

Jean got them all out into the fresh air, planted her hands on her hips and declared, "We came, we saw, we kicked its ass!"

"Ghostbusters," one of the teens said.

"Old school. Nice," the other said.

The funny thing about adrenalin is that it hits like a hammer, and the shock waves keep rolling long after that first hit. I couldn't stop myself. I reached out and grabbed Jean into a hug, one hand reaching for Myra, too, catching her shoulder.

Jean squeaked from how hard I squeezed her. Myra pulled in close, her arm extended around Jean to hold my elbow.

"We're fine," Myra said. "Delaney, we aren't hurt. None of us."

I gave Jean one more squeeze, then stepped back, letting my hands drop to my side. "Is there a fire?"

Jean glanced over her shoulder. "Well, not right now."

"Dude," a teen said. Now that I actually looked at the little group, I recognized Keith and Fernando from Crow's sale. The girl was a young dryad named Shadow, and the other teen was a non-binary human, Page, who knew all about the magical stuff in town.

They all had matching wide-eyed, utterly delighted expressions.

"So much fire," Page said.

"No heat," Shadow added. "Which was totally cool."

"And time went all…" Fernando shimmied his hands, "wibbly-wobbly."

"Right before the lightning," Keith said. "Which was… Dude."

He sounded impressed. They all did. Which was fair. Even though this was a town stuffed to the gills with magic, it wasn't every day one had a chance to see it up close.

The smoke cleared, leaving us in the cold misty air, the restless wind nibbling with needled teeth.

Fernando shivered and wrapped his arms around himself.

"You kids all okay?" I asked.

"Well, we're going to have to restart the game," Keith said. "We pushed the table over for a shield."

I glanced at Myra.

She held up the fancy red and gold box. "Hourglass. Thanks for the butterfly tip," she said to Ryder, who was right behind me, close enough he dropped his hand on my hip. It was that, his settling touch that let the rest of the adrenaline pour out of me.

"Crow figured it out," Ryder said.

"Yes," Crow picked up. "I did. You are all very welcome. I'll take money or gifts. I'm not picky."

"We don't get to keep that do we?" Page asked, tipping their head at the box.

"Nope," I said. "Sorry, it's cursed."

That got me four matching grins.

Keith whispered, "So cool."

Fernando whispered, "Worth it."

Without raising their hands, they knocked fists together, low-bones.

"Crow's going to reimburse you for it though," Jean said. "Aren't you, Crow? I mean, you sold them a cursed object. I think there's a mandatory return policy on those. Right, Ryder?"

I couldn't see Ryder since he was still standing directly behind me with his hand on my hip, but I knew he had all the laws and contracts of Ordinary burned into his brain. He had foolishly gotten himself tangled up with Mithra, god of contracts.

It made him hyperaware of the actual rules and regulations of the town. At first, he'd had a hard time ignoring it, but he'd gotten a handle on it over time, and didn't have to constantly mutter about the smallest infractions anymore.

If I never heard about another jay walker in my life, I would be thrilled.

Shadow turned her big green eyes up at Ryder. "We get our money back?" she said in a small, sweet voice. "With interest because we're just kids and we could have been killed?"

Myra had to work hard to bite back a smile, but Jean was grinning from ear to ear.

"Yeah, Crow," Jean said. "You could have killed these kids. Their parents might go all litigious when they find out. Then you're gonna be in jail for so long no one's even going to remember your name when you get out."

"No one's gonna sue me over a curse I had no knowledge of." He sauntered up to the kids, digging out his wallet. "That was what? Three bucks?"

"But we're starving," Keith said.

"Think of our mental health," Fernando added.

"The trauma, the trauma," Page said.

"Don't be a cheapskate, old man," Shadow piped up. "My miniatures got scratched up and paint ain't cheap."

I snuffed a laugh and held a thumbs up behind Crow's back.

"Lunch," Crow said, doling out bills. "Damages." He pierced Shadow with a hard look, but she just smiled. "And something left over so you can pick out a new game. Or a new timer."

He generously added a couple more bills.

"All right," Keith said nodding. "Not bad. We can live with that. Can't we, crew?"

Since Crow had dished out almost a hundred dollars, they all nodded in time.

Crow spun on his heel and scowled at me. "How's a man supposed to make a living in this town?" he grumbled.

"Oh, I don't know," I said. "But I'd start by not selling cursed property to little kids, *old man*."

"Yeah, yeah," he said, stomping back to the Jeep. "Age is a victory, you know."

"Big victory," Jean said, coming forward to throw her arm over my shoulders. "Why aren't you on vacation? You promised Myra you were leaving this morning."

"One, I promised today, not this morning. Two, maybe you've noticed there are curses on the loose?"

Myra fell into step on my other side, and Ryder followed behind us. "We got this, Delaney," Jean said. "Really. Now that we know the butterflies are the solution, we can just gather up all the items and lock them away. Easy stuff. Even a rookie could handle it."

I counted our steps against the wet pavement, the echo and rhythm of the three of us moving together as familiar as childhood.

"Things could get worse," I said.

"We know," Myra said. "We expect it will. But we have the tools to handle whatever comes up."

"For a limited time," Jean added. "Because you are still the Bridge for the god powers. None of us can take on that job."

We'd reached the vehicles now. Crow was leaning against the Jeep, his arms crossed over his chest, one sneakered foot stuck behind him on the bumper.

"Well, shit," I said. "I was supposed to be with Frigg and Than this morning."

"Power trade off?" Myra asked.

I nodded. "Can you take the toy to the station?"

"Why," Jean said moving over to lean on the Jeep next to Crow. "Did it go a little bananas?"

"Ha. Ha," Crow said.

"You love me best," she said in a sweet voice.

"I'd love you more if you had better jokes," he said in the same sweet voice.

Jean laughed and bumped her shoulder against his. He bumped her back.

"The monkey—" I started.

"—got it." Myra lifted the box out of the back of the Jeep and tucked it under her arm with the other one.

"One question," Ryder asked.

We all turned to him. Waited.

"Where did you find the butterfly sticker?"

Jean spoke up. "Myra found it stuck on the bottom of the box. They were using the box for a potato chip platter."

I exhaled a little sigh. "I can guess your next question," I said to Ryder

He nodded and tucked his hands into his jacket. "What happens if we can't find the butterfly sticker?

What happens if someone wadded it into a ball, or threw it in a fire?"

We were all silent a moment. My stomach clenched, because other than those stickers, we had no defense against the curses.

"Okay, I can stay here for at least the day. Myra, check in with our witches. See if they have any idea how to contain this stuff. I'll track down Zeus and ask him if he has any ideas, since he's been a part of Pandora's life for, like, forever."

I moved to the front door of the Jeep, put my hand on the handle.

"Or," Crow said, "we could just use these." He reached into his damp hoodie and withdrew a sheet of paper—several actually, a whole booklet—all of them covered in dozens of unused yellow butterfly stickers.

"Where did you get those?" Myra demanded.

"Score, old man!" Jean high-fived him.

"How," I shouted, louder than the others, "long have you had those things?"

Crow shrugged and tucked them safely back inside his hoodie. He pointed at Myra.

"From the storage unit. They were the last thing I found, of course."

He pointed at Jean. "Keep it up with the old man stuff, and I'll start sending everyone who goes through my shop to the other bakery instead of your boyfriend's."

Lastly, he pointed at me. "Like, since I came by your place this morning?"

"And you made me stand there holding a monkey in

my sweaty hands while you dug through the box for the old sticker? You had all those butterflies and didn't want to use one of those?"

"You're welcome, Boo Boo," he said. "I know I'm awesome."

I took a deep breath and ground my molars. "Give Jean and Myra some of those stickers. Ryder, I'll take you back to our place so you can pick up your truck. Then can you get Hatter and Shoe and Kelby some stickers, too? Just in case?"

"Yep. But that leaves you without a phone," he said.

"I'm just going over to Than's kite shop to meet with him and Frigg. I'll be fine."

Ryder held my gaze for a minute, then stepped close to me. The others headed to their vehicles, Crow deciding to ride with Jean.

"You sure you'll be okay?" he asked. He was in my space, the scent of him heady, his attention warm and hypnotizing. I couldn't take my eyes off him. Didn't want to.

"I think I really need a vacation," I breathed.

And oh, how he smiled. "Yeah, Boss," he said low and sexy. "You do. So get those god powers moved over, and I'll meet you outside the kite shop. Deal?"

"I thought you were riding with me."

"Deal?" he asked again.

"Deal."

Ryder pulled away and jogged off toward Myra. "Hey, future sister-in-law. Can I bum a ride?"

Myra, of course, already had the engine running and the door open, waiting for him.

I watched them drive off and watched the kids head back into the garage, heads together arguing about where to spend the money. And then, just as fat drops of rain began to fall, I headed off to see a god about some powers.

CHAPTER TEN

"STORM," I heard Frigg say, as the bell above the kite shop door jingled. "Bigger than last night's."

"What?" I said. I reached for my phone in my pocket, remembered it was currently dissolving in the belly of a dragon.

"Hey, Delaney," she called out cheerily from the back room. "You're late."

The sign on the door said the shop was closed. The door hadn't been locked, but with the lights turned down a bit, I was pretty sure no one would step in while we were in the middle of the freaky stuff.

God power. God power was the freaky stuff.

"Hey, Frigg." I threw the lock, just in case. "Sorry I'm late. Been chasing down some cursed objects."

Frigg leaned out so she could see through the open doorway between the front and back room. "I thought I smelled something weird. What objects?"

I strolled back. "Pandora's. A whole storage unit full of them."

"And they got out onto the street because…? she asked.

"Because Crow is a jerk."

She barked a laugh. "Oh, you are not wrong. Come sit down. We have cocoa."

I entered the back room.

Than sat with Frigg at a little round wooden table with a lace tablecloth and a plate of nuts and cheeses. A large, sterling silver decanter sat to one side with several smaller silver pots and pitchers spread out around it. The scent of chocolate and cinnamon and caramel was intense and wonderful.

"This is fancy," I said. "Are any of these going to be the container for the powers?"

Than paused with his cup and saucer halfway to his mouth. "Your imagination is staggering."

Yep. There he was. Mr. Delightful.

"Thank you. May I join?"

He waved a free hand at the open chair and I took the seat, completing the final point of the god-transfer triangle.

"Cocoa?" Than offered.

"Sure."

He turned the extra frilly china cup right side up, settling it neatly in a matching saucer.

I studied the design. "Are those… giraffes?"

He raised an eyebrow. "I believe they are."

"That's… um… some adult positions they're attempting."

"Are they not adult giraffes?"

I squinted. "Maybe?"

"Well, then."

I glanced over at Frigg, my eyes wide in a what-do-you-say-to-that expression. She slurped her cocoa, her eyes twinkling over the top of marshmallow froth.

"Mallow?" Than tugged a little silver lid off a little silver pot.

"Yes, please."

He wielded delicate engraved tongs and plunked spongy little hunks into the cup. "Whipped cream? Cinnamon? Sprinkles?"

"No, that's good. I'm all marshmallow. Ride or die."

"Fair," he granted. He passed the cup back to me, and I took it. I tried not to pay attention to which part of the giraffe was pressed against my mouth when I took a sip.

The cocoa was good. No, it was amazing. Jean would be crazy jealous if she knew Death had the best cocoa in town. I'd only found out about it because he'd invited me for a sleepover a few months ago.

"Delicious," I said.

Than inclined his head. I'd never really seen him smile, but I could tell from the light in his eyes that he was pleased.

"Okay, so the power—" I said.

"Cocoa first," Than interrupted. "Frigg and I have agreed to share this drink together to better assure the transition of power."

I looked at Frigg, expecting her to call bullshit. Drinks didn't make any difference to the powers. The only thing that made a difference was if I was there to facilitate the transfer, and if the gods involved could nominally stand each other's presence.

"First, the cocoa," Frigg insisted. "It's very good, don't you think so?"

"I just said it's delicious."

"You don't seem surprised at the quality of this beverage."

"Delicious isn't a compliment now?"

"No, no. That's not what I'm getting at. What I'm getting at is you never told me Than could brew such amazing cocoa."

I took another drink, this one deeper, catching just enough melted marshmallow to make it extra creamy.

"Maybe I was unaware of his skills," I said airily.

She chuckled. "You have been holding out on me, Reed."

"No. If Than wanted to share his cocoa, he would do so. The only person I haven't told on purpose is Jean, because she would be all over him for the recipe, and his ability to be a good reserve officer would be at risk."

"Uh-huh,"

"I was being a good friend to Than."

"Uh-huh."

"My sister can be really persistent. Annoyingly so."

"That's all part of the Reed charm," she said with a wink. "Don't you think so, Than?"

"Such charm."

"Hey. I can be charming. Very charming."

He paused and gave me his full attention. It should be a heavy thing, having the deity of death staring at me. But I could see the kindling of something a lot like humor in his eyes.

"You adore me," I insisted. "I can see it in your eyes."

"You are not even moderately charming."

"Sweet talker." I took another big gulp of cocoa, then plucked a little square of cheese up by its toothpick and popped it in my mouth.

I realized I hadn't eaten all day. I was starving.

"Where did you learn to make the cocoa?" Frigg asked.

Than looked slightly startled at how many cheese squares I was shoving in my mouth. He nudged a small empty plate my way with just the tips of his fingers as if worried I'd bite them off.

I made a happy noise and filled the plate with food.

"One cannot be an ancient god of death," Than said to Frigg, "and not have met many people as they passed through the underworld."

Frigg nodded. "Mayans?"

"Lovely people," he replied. "With rather strong opinions on how the drink should be consumed."

"I can see that. Is a second cup out of order?"

"Not at all." Than refilled her cup.

These two weren't in any kind of hurry, so I ate chunks of cheese and little round cuts of bread, olives, and cherry tomatoes until the hunger pangs were gone.

"Okay," I said, dusting my fingers on the napkin on my lap. "We need to get to the power transfer. But first, you said something about a storm?"

Frigg popped a cherry tomato in her mouth and

chewed. "Yeah. We're really going to get hammered today."

"You mean tonight?"

She frowned. "Didn't you get the emergency weather update?"

"My phone's broken."

"Oh, I thought you knew. Here." She pulled her phone out of her pocket, unlocked the screen, tapped it, and handed it to me.

I read through the National Weather Service update. We had a winter storm rolling in on us faster and harder than they'd forecasted yesterday. We'd have sustained winds at seventy miles per hour and gusts well over a hundred miles per hour.

"Well, crap." I rubbed at my forehead. "All right. I need to check in with everyone, make sure we're as prepared for this as we can be."

Frigg took her phone back. "What about that vacation?"

I bit my bottom lip. I really wanted that vacation.

"I want to go."

"You should." She reached over and patted my hand. "What did you decide on?"

"Cabin in the mountains."

"Oh," she said, knowing what I'd already figured out.

The storm we'd had last night had dropped a lot of snow in the mountains. The one tonight would mean closing the passes.

If Ryder and I wanted a chance at the hot tub, at peace and quiet, just the two of us, solitude at a little cabin out in the middle of nowhere, we'd need to leave now. Or as close to now as possible.

"Well?" Than asked.

"Well what?"

"Are you going on vacation, or are you going to let a minor weather event stop you?"

"It's not minor."

He waved one hand. "In the history of storms, it will not deserve an asterisk's worth of ink."

"Weather won't stop me," I said. "But I'm not going to be stupid either. Driving into a blizzard is stupid."

"There's no blizzard yet. Passes are still open," Frigg said.

"Perhaps if you hurried?" Than suggested.

I closed my eyes for an extra beat. "I have been hurrying. It's you two cocoa freaks who are dawdling."

"That's true," Frigg said. "I am a cocoa freak. So are you ready to get this show on the road?"

"I am," Than said.

"Do you have the vessel?" I asked.

"I do," he said.

"And you, Frigg, do you have the porting vessel?"

"Right here." She plopped the bobbin from her spinning wheel onto the table like this was a game of poker and she'd just upped the ante. "Let's see it," she challenged.

Than took his time placing all the little silver pots on a tray. He rose and settled them behind him. Next was the carafe. Then he brushed off the tablecloth, and finally, he sat back in the chair.

"What are you going to use for—" I asked, but

stopped suddenly when, with a flourish of his hand, he deposited the vessel he intended to use for carrying all the resting god powers onto the table.

The silence became a living thing.

"That's a toy."

"You have keen observation skills, Reed Daughter."

I studied his face. "You're serious? This is what you want to use to hold all the powers?"

"I was told it should be easily hidden, durable, and if possible, portable."

That was true. All of it. "Is this durable enough?"

Than raised one eyebrow. "It is more than it appears to be, Reed Daughter."

"Delaney," I absently corrected. "It better be. Because this looks like the Grim Reaper stuffy Jean gave you."

I didn't dare touch it, but the little stuffed toy stared up at me with its big, green, sparkling eyes, fluffy, black-cowled robe, stitched-on smile, and a wee scythe clasped in its tiny white hands.

"I think it's adorable," Frigg said. "It's nothing anyone would expect to hold power which makes it perfect. Let's do this." She tapped the tabletop with a fingertip.

"Now you're in a hurry?" I teased.

She shrugged. "That storm is going to mean plenty of tow jobs. And I want to get some grocery shopping in before it hits."

"Milk and bread?"

"Storm staples," she agreed. "So if you're okay with all this?" She waved at the toy and Than.

I nodded. "You're sure this is where you want to keep all the powers?" I asked, giving Than one more chance to change his mind.

"If it is insufficient, I will adjust when it is once again my turn in the rotation," he said.

"Okay," I said, "that can work. You made sure it can withstand the powers?"

"I may be new to guarding these powers, Reed Daughter, but I am a very old god."

"Which is neat, but hey, a yes or no will make all the difference here."

"Yes," he said very clearly. "It will withstand the powers."

The rain rattled against the roof and windows, just a scattering of drops. But I knew it was going to become a deluge soon.

"All right." I squared my shoulders and took a deep breath. There wasn't really a ritual or ceremony for this. Usually, the other deities liked to come and watch, because they were judgmental about how their own power was handled by other gods.

"No one wanted to be here?" I asked Frigg.

"I put out the call and no one replied."

I nodded and got on with it. "Than, do you promise to guard and keep hidden the god powers of Ordinary for the whole of one year?"

"Yes, Reed Daughter."

"Will you allow any deity to come to your shop, allow them to see their power, or reclaim their power at any time, day or night, as long as you are present?"

"Yes."

137

I nodded. "Frigg?"

She picked up the bobbin, held it between her palms and whispered something beyond my understanding that sounded like spring's thread weaving through winter's warp.

Then she tipped the bobbin in her fingers and it pointed down toward the fuzzy little Reaper.

Powers aren't liquid and don't follow the rules of gravity. But they do follow the will of the gods. If Frigg wanted the powers to pour out of the bobbin, they were going to pour out.

I didn't see power, not the way my father had. But here, with so many mingled together, they filled my vision, bright and burning—twisted ropes, strings, cords —vibrant and alive.

But the song of god powers, that, I could hear. It rose, filling the room, filling the world, filling me with a wild, driving melody that soared to horizons and realities beyond my imagination.

Voices called: laughter, passion, singing, shouting. Lyrics slipped jewel-bright through the song, weaving between life and death, the poetry of creation carved upon each rush and ebb.

Power strummed over my skin, stretching my breath, zinging through my bones like sweet lighting until I was the sky, the void, the silver-shot stars with only a single, thin, crystalline thread connecting me to this earth.

It was heady.

It was overwhelming.

It was wonderful.

Then there was *here* and *yes* and *home, home, home,* the

song fading and fading as the powers settled, quieted, and were once again at rest.

"You okay, Delaney?" Frigg asked.

I blinked until my eyes could focus on the little room again, waiting for the afterimages of those massive powers to disappear.

"Good," I croaked, as I accepted the glass of water she handed me and gulped it down. "It's always such an experience."

She patted me on the shoulder. "Thank you for making time for this today."

"Sure," I said. "No problem. You headed out?"

"Yep." She snagged up the bobbin and dropped it into her pocket. Then she stood. "You okay here? Both of you?"

I looked at Than who sat exactly across from me. His hands were folded on the table in front of him, long, bony fingers slotted together, just inches short of touching the little Reaper toy.

Than's expression was unreadable, but his eyes burned with dark flame.

"I'm okay," I said. "Than?"

His face shifted, just slightly, the corners of his eyes relaxing, the skin near his mouth smoothing. "I, too, am well. Shall I see you out, Frigg?"

"Naw. I can see the door from here. So I'll just leave you to it. Later, babes!" She strolled out of the room, her boots solid on the old wooden floor, the click of the lock shifting, the bell over the door tinkling.

Then she was gone, leaving nothing behind but a fresh swirl of salty air.

I waited a minute or so, but Than just stared at the stuffed toy, not even breathing.

"Do we need to talk?" I asked.

He inhaled, exhaled, and something seemed to settle in the room, like the barometric pressure, or gravity, or the god of death who was now looking after every other power in town.

"We could," he said. "Is there something you wish to speak about?"

"How are you feeling about the powers?" I nodded toward the stuffy.

His gaze swung down to the toy, then back to me. "It is... not a feeling that is important. Rather the uniqueness of these powers coexisting without massive destruction is... interesting."

"Interesting?"

"Refreshing."

"That sounds good."

"It is."

I blew out a breath. "Good. For a minute there I thought you were going to go back on the deal and tell me to find someone else to watch over the powers."

He *tsk*ed, then plucked up the toy and carried it as if it didn't weigh anything, as if it didn't carry the powers of reality and destruction, over to his desk. He placed it right back on the same shelf I'd seen it on yesterday.

"I gave you my word." He turned back around. "Whatever have I done to make you assume I had no follow through?"

I grinned. "Nothing. Thanks for that. And thanks for this. Looking after the powers."

"Yes, well, it is required for one to live in Ordinary, and I see no reason to leave."

"Because you like me," I teased, standing up and helping stack cups.

He made another small sound.

"Because you like Ordinary," I pressed.

This time he gave me a tolerant look.

"And you like that Tala is here now and wants to be your girlfriend."

"Aren't you running late for a vacation Delaney Reed? Somewhere out of town and out of cell service?"

I chuckled. "Why? You tired of me already?"

"You have no idea." But those eyes of his. They were all sparkle, sparkle, sparkle.

"Say, I was wondering," I said, as we carried the dishes to the little sink in the corner. "Can I ask you a favor?"

"Other than keeping the powers for a year?"

"Yeah, other than that."

"Yes."

"I've been trying to figure out who to ask to watch the dragon pig while I'm gone."

"I see."

"I was going to leave it to Myra, but she'll be taking over most of my job duties at the station when I'm gone. I know she won't let it into the library, so if she needs to do a research project, there will be no one to keep an eye on it."

"Obviously."

"Jean could take it, and she asked to, but she has her

hands full dealing with the demon-farm-animal-love-triangle thing with Xtelle, Amy, and Pan."

"Of course," he said.

"And I know it's a dragon in pig shape, so it doesn't actually need a keeper, but I'd feel better if someone could make sure it doesn't eat something important."

"Important?"

"Yeah, like a building."

"Noted."

I waited, hoping I'd put out enough bait. I had no idea if Than and the dragon would get along for any length of time, but there was one other benefit to dragon-sitting. I hoped he'd caught onto what it might be.

"And what of the dog?"

Bingo.

"Spud?" I asked like he hadn't even crossed my mind. "I guess I'll need someone to look after him too. He does love being with the dragon pig, though."

"I see."

"They're practically inseparable. I'd hate for Spud to have to spend a week all alone without his dragon pig buddy. But really, it's too much to ask one person to take on responsibility for both critters."

"Yes. It is too much."

"Oh. But will you at least watch the dragon pig? Poor Spud is going to be so lonely locked away in the rent-a-kennel place."

"You are an abysmally poor actor, Reed Daughter."

"Hey! I'm great—I mean, I wasn't acting."

"Yes, to the dragon and to the dog."

"You'll watch them both?"

He sighed like I was just the most annoying thing in the universe. I had to bite back a smile.

"Yes. Both."

"Thank you!"

"And in return, you will owe me a favor of my asking."

"Wait. No. That's not how... Maybe I could ask Hatter..."

"No. You will not ask any other, since I have agreed. But now you owe me, Reed Daughter."

"You did that on purpose," I said.

"Whatever are you talking about?"

"You made me think I was manipulating you into watching the dog and dragon and really you wanted to ask me a favor."

"I have no idea what you're talking about."

"What's the favor?"

"I haven't decided yet."

"Mean," I said, though I didn't really mean it. "This vacation better be worth it."

He crossed his arms over his chest. "You will never know until you actually take it."

"I know. I'm going. I am. But there are a bunch of cursed items out there."

"I heard."

"Probably more than Crow told me."

"Undoubtedly."

"It's hard," I said. He waited while I sorted my thoughts. "Hard to leave everyone else behind to mop up the mess."

"Life is messy, Delaney Reed. So is Ordinary. That's rather the point."

I grinned, because he wasn't wrong.

The door jangled and we both looked. Ryder glanced around the shop, his gaze taking in all the whimsical, predatory kites.

"Laney?" he called out. "You here?"

"In the back," I said. Then, to Than: "Thank you." I stepped forward and, on a whim, hugged him.

Hugging the god of death was a little like wrapping ones arms around a glacier, a stalagmite, the emptiness of the void. He was cool to the touch, hard, and didn't move a millimeter.

"This is the part where you wrap your arms around me too," I muttered into his shoulder. "It's called a hug."

Finally, his arms moved and crossed together behind my back. "I know what a hug is," he muttered into the side of my hair.

I squeezed him once and stepped back. "Couldn't tell," I said. "I think you might need more practice."

He wasn't blushing. I'd never seen him blush. But there was higher color under his skin. I thought he might be pleased.

"Perhaps I do," he allowed. "Mr. Bailey," he said, looking over my shoulder. "I understand you and Delaney are leaving on vacation soon."

"No," Ryder said. "I think that's off the table now."

The rough tremor in his voice caught my attention. He was freaked out, his eyes wide, his hand, where it was braced on the wall, shaking.

He wasn't just freaking out, he was terrified.

"What happened?" I ran to him, looking for blood, frightened that he was hurt and how bad it must be.

My emotions were all over the place, and my brain seemed to grind to a halt.

"Are you hurt?" I pressed my hands to his hands, to his arms, to his face.

"No, I'm fine. But we have to go. We have to get out there and help them." He gripped my wrist and yarded me out of the shop.

The wind slapped cold and sharp, the gusts shattering rain.

"What?" I said, running to keep pace with him. "Help with what?"

"It's on the beach," he said. "Cursed. Item. Beach."

"Are Myra and Jean there? Are they in danger? What item?"

"Yes, yes." He threw open the passenger door to his truck and shoved me in before sprinting around to get behind the wheel.

Spud and the dragon pig were in the back seat. Spud barked once, excited about whatever it was that was making his man act so crazy. But the dragon pig growled.

I'd never heard it growl like that. Not even for demons.

"It's okay," I said, even though I was trying to think of what could be worse than demons. "It is okay, isn't it?" I asked Ryder.

He had the truck in gear and was high-tailing it down the back roads, aiming for a beach access that would allow us to drive out onto the sand.

"I don't know. It's huge." His eyes were still too wide, his color off.

"Okay. It's going to be okay. What is it? What's the cursed item?

He took a hard right and barreled down the paved beach access, out over the river stones, and onto the sand.

"Holy hell," I said, my hand tightening on the dash as I braced for the bumpy ride.

There, rising out of the ocean, storm clouds whipping behind it, was a creature so huge so…monstrous it stole my breath.

"It's a…"

"… sea monster," Ryder said, slamming on the brakes next to Myra's cruiser and Jean's truck. "It's a sea monster."

CHAPTER ELEVEN

"TECHNICALLY," I said, "it's an ocean monster because seas are smaller bodies of water partially surrounded by land."

"What is it doing here?" he asked, a little too loudly.

Sea monsters—ocean monsters—never came to Ordinary.

Was this beast here to become a citizen of the town? If so, why hadn't it come in some sort of disguise? People must have seen it by now. It was massive. And angry.

I mean, everyone had a cell phone. Anyone could snap a photo of that monstrosity.

Or livestream a video.

Shit.

Someone might even be doing that right now.

"No, no, no!" I opened the door and ran out onto the beach.

The weather was worse. Wind and rain mixed with

saltwater and sand lashed at my exposed skin until it was red and stinging.

The only good thing about this weather was that no one was stupid enough to be down on the beach.

Except for us. We were the stupid ones.

I could just make out the shapes of Myra and Bathin, Jean and Hogan, and Crow, all of them a couple hundred yards away on the tide's edge.

I ran across the hard sand toward them, the smell of kelp, salt and deeper, meatier things sharp in my nose, my boot prints filling with water instantly after each step.

The ocean crashed in my ears, and that monster roared like multiple, smaller, stormier oceans. My heartbeat settled into the run.

Running was good. This motion, this Zen of my body falling into my running stride cleared my thoughts. Logic snicked into place.

Yes, there was a monster in the ocean.

Yes, it looked like a super-sized cross between a giant squid and a multi-headed Loch Ness monster. Yep, there were lots of brownish-red tentacles sprouting around three long-necked plesiosaur heads, all of them sporting huge, filmy yellow eyes and massive, jagged teeth.

Yes, it was probably being caught on film right this minute and uploaded to some cloud storage somewhere.

But it hadn't come ashore yet. Hadn't destroyed any buildings or eaten anyone.

Which, really, was a point in the "good" column.

I had no idea how to talk to it, or get rid of it, or kill it (an image of an exploding, rotted whale flashed behind my eyes), but my sisters were both already facing off against that huge monster. Myra with a spell book in her hand. Jean with a bullhorn and mallet.

Crow was there too, hands on his hips, head tipped up, scowling at the beast.

Then, even as I closed the distance, blinking away the stinging rain and sand, I saw Bathin, who was a demon, next to Myra, nodding as she read out of the book. Hogan, Jean's boyfriend, who was part Jinn, had his arm looped around her waist, an anchor, holding her tight.

I was almost there, my heart in each footstep, my thoughts a mantra: *please let them stay, please don't let them be hurt, please let me get to them in time.*

Then: motion.

Coming down the cliff side, over layered basalt ridges and tough knolls of sea grass, were dozens of people. No, not people, werewolves and vampires.

The entire Rossi clan flowed over that cliff like a wave of black, Old Rossi in the lead, his lean, blade-thin body cutting through the wind like the edge of midnight against a liquid dawn.

Rumbling right behind the vamps was a mob of muscle. At least three dozen werewolves powered across the rock and sand. Granny Wolfe, small and quick and way too old to be moving that fast, led the charge.

No one had shifted into wolves. The vampires still looked human and so did the werewolves, but they were all moving at a speed no human could match.

Moving toward the edge of the ocean.

More cars drove onto the sand and spilled out

various gods and goddesses. None of them were carrying their powers, but I could tell by how they were marching this way that they were pissed off.

They were not about to let an ocean monster ruin their vacation time.

Just before I made it to Jean, just before I could ask her how this had happened and what we could do to stop it, she shouted into the bullhorn.

"Now, Chris, now!"

I pulled up short and spun on my heel, expecting a monster attack. But instead, I saw a flash of black dive through the stormy gray and white waves.

Chris Lagon, our local gilman.

He was the owner of Jump Off Jack's, an award-winning craft brewery. But right now he didn't look like a businessman. No, he looked like black lightning: fast and deadly and sleek.

He swam through the curl of waves, closing in on the ocean monster.

The Hollywood creature from the black lagoon couldn't hold a candle to the real deal. Chris was built for this, his body a bullet, his arms and legs cutting through the chop like he was taking a dip in a summer-smooth pond.

The ocean monster spotted Chris and roared again, all three heads tracking the gilman. The monster thrashed, tentacles falling from a great height, hitting the water with earth-shaking *boom*s, each slap a crack of thunder, a rolling earthquake.

Chris just kept swimming, diving and ducking the whip-fast tentacles. He narrowly missed being grabbed and dragged to the bottom of the ocean, once, twice. Again and again.

Jean yelled, "Do it! Do it!" and Chris dove beneath the waves, shooting into the barrel of a massive curl.

He popped out the other side, but instead of avoiding the tentacle slapping down to grab him, he pushed up, jumped out of the water and landed on his feet—on top of the tentacle.

He sprinted the length of the twisting, knotted appendage, headed toward the triple necks.

I had good eyes, but I couldn't see what happened through that much spray and rain.

One minute Chris was running, his fist cocked back like he was going to punch the ocean monster in the neck. A huge wave lifted, blocking my view.

Then the next minute, the monster roared. Tentacles whipped wildly as it sank down and down beneath the waves, the ocean swallowing it up: suckers, necks, and heads until, finally, it was gone.

Jean swung the bullhorn toward Crow and yelled, "Ha! I told you so!"

He clapped one hand over his ear. "I still think a dart gun or slingshot would have been more fun."

"Did that really happen?" Ryder had caught up with me and now stood with his shoulder against mine, staring at the water.

"Like you would have been able to hit it from here," Jean shouted through the bullhorn again. Then she noticed the crowd of gods and weres and vamps streaming onto the beach.

Unfortunately, human citizens were coming down to the sand too.

She turned toward the crowd of people standing near the shoreline. "Okay, it's okay everyone. Everything's fine."

"Did he just punch a sea monster to death?" Ryder asked, sounding dazed.

"Ocean monster," I corrected absently.

One of the gods snickered, the vampires all moved in to make sure there weren't any bits of beast evidence washing up on shore, and the werewolves all strode out to the shoreline, instantly falling into crowd control mode.

Crow spotted me and came strolling up.

"Delaney Reed. Whatever are you doing out in this miserable weather?"

"What the hell happened, Crow?"

"How long have you been standing there?"

"Long enough to see a sea monster get its ass kicked by Chris."

"Ocean monster," Ryder added.

"Then you're up to date on everything that's happened," Crow said. "Good talk."

"Spill," I said, grabbing the sleeve of his hoodie. "What. Happened?"

"It was a cursed item," Ryder said.

Crow pointed at him.

"How do you know?" I asked Ryder.

"Got the call. Came for you."

Myra and Jean both walked over. The rain wasn't any better and the wind was worse. It made standing here no fun at all. Myra wiped her hand over her face, the book already tucked away safely in her waterproof satchel.

"What was it?" I asked.

"A denizen of the sea," Myra said. "Not an eldritch abomination, but one of the unnamed monsters of the watery void."

"Huh," Ryder said. "Watery void monster."

"And it was here why?" I asked.

"This." We all turned to see Chris Lagon jogging up to us. He had a wide grin on his face and looked like he'd just had the time of his life.

Chris had worked magic into his tattoos so that most people saw his scales as part of the intricate, beautifully inked designs, and otherwise ignored the slight differences that marked him as gilman instead of human.

But here, after a strenuous swim in the ocean, a fight with a monster, and now, a jog in the rain and wind, he looked wilder. His long hair streamed in dark rivers over his shoulders and back. Even the magic in his tattoos couldn't dampen his natural form.

"Pandora thing." He handed me what I, at first, thought was a collection of sticks.

They were not sticks but rather delicately carved pieces of wood linked together with what looked like chains of gold. I shifted them to figure out how they all connected and realized it was a child's mobile, the arms of which were a giant squid. Hanging from each tentacle were little Nessie monsters and jelly fish.

Smack dab on the neck of one of the three Nessies was a familiar yellow butterfly sticker.

"Who had it?" I asked.

"Molly." Myra took it from me and dropped it into a red and gold box before tucking it in her bag.

"Your waitress?" I asked Chris.

He nodded. "She wanted to hang it up at Jump Off's. I liked it and said yes."

"And when she took off the sticker?" I asked.

Chris shook his head. "I took it off, like an idiot. I thought it felt like magic, but I couldn't be sure. And then, bang. Big-ass monster."

"Bang," Ryder echoed. "Big-ass monster."

"Is everyone okay?" I asked. "Is your brewery still standing?"

"Everyone's fine," he said. "The curse called forth a monster from the watery void, and luckily that watery void was out here offshore instead of in my kitchen sink. Hey, weren't you going on vacation this morning?"

Myra handed him a shirt and Jean just scoffed. "Oh, yeah, she's so into vacationing. Can't you tell?"

Chris nodded and shimmied into the shirt. "I can tell."

"We're gathering quite the crowd," Ryder said. "How are we going to convince the humans they didn't see what they just saw?"

Myra looked to me, I looked to the gods all standing in their own huddle. They made a point of pretending they hadn't been eavesdropping on us. Probably didn't want to volunteer to pick up their powers for something this small, since that would mean they'd have to leave Ordinary, and their vacations, for a year.

"I got this," Jean said. "Boyfriend?" she asked Hogan. "Would you grant me a wish?"

Hogan still had his arm around her waist. "You know I'd do anything for you, babe. But there's a limit on wishes. You sure you want to use one now?"

She tipped her head up and fluttered her lashes. "Can we negotiate later? Tonight? In bed? When I do that thing with my mouth that you—"

He clamped his hand over her mouth, and if his skin hadn't been so dark, and it hadn't been raining so hard, I would have sworn he was blushing.

"What's your wish?" he asked. "Be specific."

He dropped his hand and Jean straightened a bit, thinking through what she was going to say.

He stood in front of her, both hands on her upper arms, catching her gaze. "You got this. You totally got this."

She nodded. "All right. I wish that all the humans of Ordinary who do not know about the gods and magic and supernaturals in the town, and those among them who saw, or took pictures or video of the monster, no longer remember the monster."

"And," he encouraged.

"And they instead saw… a storm and big waves and crashing water and driftwood in the waves. Maybe a whale. And," she added, her voice going up in a question, "the pictures they took and videos are all deleted?"

"That's *very* specific," he said.

"But you can do that?"

"As you wish." He gave her a little bow.

Aw. Movie quote love.

Jean's smile softened and she gazed at him like he hung the moon. "I am *so* gonna do that thing you like with my mouth tonight." She breathed out dreamily.

He chuckled then turned to me. "I don't grant her wishes all the time."

"That's good."

"Most of her wishes are just little things."

"Okay."

"Food things. Bedroom things."

"Didn't need to know that last part."

"If I were ever going to grant a really big wish, I'd run it past you or Myra first."

"Hogan," I said. "I am one hundred percent in favor of you granting my sister's wish. Now would be good."

Relief smoothed his face into a smile. Hogan wasn't someone who liked to throw his magic around. Wishes could be dangerous.

"All right," he said, rubbing his hands together. "Let's grant this thing." He recited something silently, his mouth moving, his eyes closed. Then he clapped his hands together hard. Once. Twice.

Wishes were tricky magic. They weren't flashy like curses or showy like spells. They were more of a gift, a boon. They were hope inherent: the sound of an ice cream truck pulling up to the curve, the glow of birthday candles right before they became smoke, a love letter unopened.

This wish manifested as a pause in the rain. The wind slowed to a warm summer swirl; clouds pulled apart to reveal a patch of blue that allowed one sweet, golden spear of sunlight to scatter across the waves.

The crowd which had been restless and loud, held very still.

Someone laughed, someone else whistled, and then the blue sky was swallowed, the rain sifted down, and the wind buffeted us all.

The moment had passed, the event was over, and I was confident the people in town who were unaware of magic were now convinced they'd seen a stormy ocean, driftwood, and maybe a whale.

Too bad none of their pictures or videos would be viable.

"I love it when you do that," Jean said. "Makes me all shivery."

Hogan had his arms around her and kissed her on the mouth, quick. "You're welcome."

"Is that it?" Ryder asked. "Did it work?"

Chris tipped his head to one side like he was trying to get water out of his ear. "Yup. He's good."

"Thanks, Hogan," I said. "You're a lifesaver."

"No problem."

"And thank you, too, Chris," I said. "That would have been a nightmare without you out in the water."

"Happy to do it," he said. "Anyone want to warm up and get a beer? On me."

That got everyone's attention. More than half the gods were up for it, and the vamps were suddenly all headed his way. So were the werewolves now that they and the weather had sent the crowd packing.

Chris was carried away in a crowd of weres and vamps and gods.

Crow, Myra and Bathin, Jean and Hogan, and Ryder and I all walked back to our vehicles.

"Wanna go get a beer?" Jean asked, yelling over the wind. "I mean until the next curse hits?"

"You're on duty," Myra yelled back.

Jean tipped her face to the stormy sky and howled a silent, "Why!" then spit salty rain out of her mouth. She tipped her head back down. "Right. Of course. And I love my job! Love working outside in a storm. Love my wet socks. Love my wet bra."

Myra laughed. "We can get out of the weather. If another sticker is removed, we'll see the beam of light."

"You still going with electric lines?" Bathin asked.

"Yes," she said. "The power outages make a perfect cover story. Why?"

He shrugged. "You know if you wanted a little demon mojo, I'm more than happy to lend you my services."

Myra gave him an arch look. "I think adding demon mojo to an avalanche of curses might not be the safest way to go, don't you agree?"

"Oh, baby, since when do you drive in the safe lane?"

Even in the dim light, I could see my sister blush. "No mojo," she admonished.

He crossed his chest. "Hope to die."

"That's not where your heart is."

He winked and ducked down into the passenger side of the cruiser.

Hogan had swung up into Jean's truck, and I was

next to Ryder at the door of his, but both my sisters and Crow were still standing out in the storm, looking at me.

"What's the play, Chief?" Myra asked.

"Well, I for one, am going for that beer," Crow said.

"No," all three of us Reeds said.

"This is your mess," I said. "You finish the clean up."

"Clean it up. Stay away. You girls have got to make up your mind," he grouched.

"You go with Myra," I said, and she nodded. "Jean, is Hogan staying with you?"

"Yep."

"Okay, so you're covering south side of the city. Think you can call in Kelby or Hatter or Shoe to cover central?"

She frowned, "Kelby's available. Maybe Than?"

"Yeah, they could team up. Myra, you and Crow can take north."

They were all silent for a second.

"What part of town are you taking?" Crow asked with an innocent lilt that was totally fake.

"No part." I grabbed Ryder's hand, and it was warm and somehow dry. "I'm going on vacation."

CHAPTER TWELVE

A FLASH of yellow lit up the rearview mirror, the earth to sky beam massive and thick before it winked out of existence.

"We can turn around," Ryder said, as he slowed the truck.

"I know."

"It's another cursed object."

"I know. But they've got it covered. Everyone in town has it covered."

"You sure? The place might be a mess by the time we get back."

"That's okay. Life is messy. So is Ordinary."

He shot me a glance, then stretched his hand out over the console toward me. "It's going to be okay."

"It is." I waited, because I could tell he was just bursting with the need to tell me all about the cabin he'd rented. "So," I said. "Tell me about the place you picked."

SEALED WITH A TRYST

He exhaled and grinned. "You sure you want to know? Or would you rather it be a surprise?"

"We've got four hours of driving—"

"—at least five—"

"—at least five hours of driving, and we're trying to shoot the gap between storms. Talk to me, Ryder. Tell me about our first vacation place together."

"For starters, it has no monsters."

I laughed. "I like it already."

"And it's out past the Three Sisters, in the middle of nowhere facing a fir grove with a stream."

"Pretty."

"Solitude. It's going to be peaceful and quiet. Just the two of us, a hot tub, some wine, and the falling snow."

I sighed and leaned my head against the window. That sounded perfect. I had to stretch my arm a bit to keep hold of his hand, but I was fine with that. More than fine with that because I didn't want to let go.

"What else?" I asked, feeling my eyes close. It had been a long day, a long winter. Hell, it had been a long year. Just knowing that I didn't have to save anyone, protect anything, or bear the responsibilities of gods, supernaturals, and humans for a few days made me feel light. Like I was floating.

My head bumped something hard, and I woke up with a snort. "Whatsit?"

"Just the road," Ryder said. "Didn't mean to wake you."

"No. It's okay," I said taking stock of my surroundings. Ryder had tossed the Pendleton blanket over my lap and one shoulder. The radio was low, playing a soft Pink Floyd song about earthbound misfits. The world around us was pure, bracing white.

"Snow," I said, unnecessarily.

"Yep."

"Wow. It's really coming down."

"We're still on the leading edge of the storm." He pointed at his cell. "It's going to really hit and hunker down in about an hour."

"How long until the cabin?"

"About an hour." He slid me a grin.

"You do like to live an exciting life, Ryder Bailey."

"I do. Now that you're awake, would you pour us some coffee? Thermos is there at your feet, and snacks are in that bag."

"Look at you, thinking of everything. Front seat picnic. I like it." I refilled his travel mug and mine, then dug around until I found the chocolate and chips.

"So you like it so far?" Ryder asked. "Our vacation?"

I held up coffee in one hand and a candy bar in the other. "What's not to like?"

"Okay, okay, good. I just really want you to like it."

"I'll really like it."

"No matter how it turns out."

"As long as it's you and me and solitude and in the middle of nowhere, it's gonna be perfect. Heaven."

"Better than bungee jumping?"

I almost spit my coffee. "Anything's better than bungee jumping. What were you thinking?"

"Got your attention, didn't it?"

"Sure, but how is stepping off a cliff a good vacation activity?"

"If you stepped off a cliff, I'd be right behind you."

"Aw, that's sweet."

He puffed out his chest looking proud of himself.

"And stupid."

He deflated, but there was still a little smile on his face. "You thought it was romantic."

"No, I didn't."

"For a second you did. Just like you think this little tryst is romantic."

"Is that what this is, a tryst?"

"It's going to be private, it's going to be romantic, and we are lovers, so yes, I'd say this is the very definition of a tryst."

"I'm just glad there won't be any more brochures."

"You liked those too. Plus, I was very subtle."

"You taped them to the bathroom mirror."

"Yeah."

"You left them all over the refrigerator."

"Yeah."

"You left them *in* the refrigerator."

"It worked, didn't it?"

"No." I took a sip of coffee, then said, "Yes."

"Good. Now look for our turn off. The owners said they'd stick an orange traffic cone on either side of the road."

I peered into the falling snow. It was almost dark, and the clouds made it darker. The towering ponderosa and jack pines were smothered in white, their branches drooping heavily from the weight of the snow. There were several vehicles in front of us: three eighteen wheelers trying to get their deliveries through, a truck like the one we were in, and one tiny compact that was tailgating the snowplow.

Oregon was a state of mountains and ranges and hills and canyons. When snow hit, and hit hard, the roads were dangerous enough that the passes were closed a few times a year.

"What if we get snowed in?" I asked.

"Extra vacation days? Think you can handle it?"

Yeah, I thought I could. It might take me a few days to let go of being the go-to problem solver, but I was determined to relax, really relax, even if it killed me.

"There." I pointed at the turn off, and Ryder tapped the brakes, bringing our already slow progress to a crawl.

He guided the truck into the turn, and we quickly left the narrow four-lane highway behind. The jack and ponderosa pines here were closer to the skinny two-lane road. Snow had piled outward from each shoulder, narrowing the road even further.

"How will we know our place?" I asked.

"It's a few miles in, after a little bridge."

A few miles took a lot longer at the speed we were going, but we finally crossed the bridge.

The little cabin was a gorgeous, compact A-frame made of big, beautiful old logs. The porch was tucked out of the weather and had a lovely hand-carved bench beside the door.

"This is it!" Ryder pulled the truck alongside the cabin. "What do you think?"

His eyes were bright with excitement, and his lips were swollen because he'd been worrying at them during the drive.

All I wanted to do was kiss him and get him in bed. Naked. With me.

"What are you thinking about right now, soon-to-be Mrs. Bailey-Reed?" he asked.

"Hyphenate, huh? You think so?" I reached over and tugged on the collar of his flannel.

"Well, you do have this family name to live up to. All those Reeds in history doing all that fancy god power stuff."

"You think I'm fancy?"

He was leaning close, closer. I was stretching out to him, turning so I didn't have to fight my seatbelt.

"I think you're the most amazing thing in the universe," he said.

His eyes were so close to mine, I could see the nebula array of stars there, in greens and golds. So close, I could see my heart reflected in them.

"I love you," I said. Before he could reply, I took his mouth and claimed him as mine, telling him with touch, with taste, with desire, that he was all I needed. Telling him he couldn't leave me because we were just at the beginning of this thing called us, just at the beginning of our lives together.

I wanted years and years of it.

With him.

Only him.

"Wow," he said. "I'm taking you out into the middle of nowhere more often."

"Good," I said, kissing him once more just because I could. "See that you do that."

I opened the door and full-on girly-shrieked from the cold. "You have the key, right?"

He handed me his phone. "Lock box code right there."

I jumped out, glad I was still wearing my work boots, but wishing I'd added a scarf and gloves. I pulled a beanie out of my pocket and stuck it on my head, pulling it over my ears. Then I made a dash for the door.

Snow smacked cold kisses against my cheeks, nose, and chin. The air smelled crisp and fresh and clean. I "*eek*ed" again, just to hear Ryder laugh.

He was out of the truck, slamming open the tailgate. There was the sound of luggage dragging across the truck bed, then *thunk*ing into the snow, grocery bags rustling around.

I punched in the numbers, excited for the moment, excited for the experience.

Just Ryder and me.

No dragon pig or Spud to take care of—though I would probably miss them.

No gods to keep in line.

No supernaturals to guide.

No people to look after.

No Valkyrie and her never-ending community events.

As long as the heat worked and the roof didn't leak, everything about this was going to be perfect.

Solitude.

Just the two of us.

Heaven.

I lifted the latch but waited until the *crunch-crunch-crunch* of Ryder's footsteps came near.

"Everything okay?" he asked, as he stomped snow off the soles of his boots.

"Just waiting for you. Ready?"

He smiled. "Ready."

I pushed open the door and stepped through.

The first thing that hit me was the wall of windows filling the entire back side of the cabin from floor to pointed peak.

After that, I noted the deck, the hot tub just a few steps up on a second, connected deck, and the snow-covered trees surrounding it. Beyond the trees, I caught a glimpse of the circular clearing below, and the still flowing stream winding through it.

"Oh," I said, breathing out the word. "This is wonderful."

Ryder stepped up behind me and wrapped his arms around mine.

"You like?"

"Very much."

He kissed the top of my head. "Good. Because we have a lot of unpacking to do."

CHAPTER THIRTEEN

TURNED OUT I LIKED VACATIONS. Who knew? The unpacking had been quick and would have been quicker if Ryder hadn't put his face in the way of the snowball I was totally just randomly throwing in his general direction.

Cue one massive snowball fight.

"Which I totally won!" I said, flicking hot tub water at Ryder's face.

"The best fiancé in the world prize?" Ryder asked, unperturbed by his wet face. "Yes. Yes, you did."

"No. The snowball fight. I won it."

He raised one eyebrow and tipped back his wine glass. "You must be drunk. You lost."

I was not drunk. Maybe a little floaty, but it would take more than one glass of wine after that fabulous roast we'd had for dinner to get me anywhere near drunk territory.

"Lies." More wine sounded good, so I tipped back my glass. It was empty, darn it. "I can tell when anyone is lying, Ryder Bailey. I am an officer of the law and have a finely honed bullshit meter. I won that fight fair and square."

"No," he shifted forward and all the water in the hot tub sloshed, some of it pitching over the edge to land on the snowy deck. "I distinctly remember sitting on you and pinning your arms until you cried uncle."

"Yes, but I let you."

"You let me smash snow in your face?"

"It only seemed fair with how badly you were losing."

He crowded up in front of me, his hands slipping under the water to curve against my ribs before running down my waist to my stomach, my thighs.

"Mmmm," I hummed, pushing my arms out of the water to drape them along the tub's ledge. "That's nice. Come here."

"I am here." His hands wandered and I fought the urge to arch my back into his touch.

"Come closer here," I said.

He moved in closer, his pupils blown wide, his mouth soft. I loved that look on him. Like he was staring at the one thing in the world he desired, and that one thing was me.

He bent his head to kiss my neck, and I scooped up a huge handful of snow and smooshed it against the back of his head.

He howled. I scrabbled out from under him as fast as I could move.

He dunked under to get rid of the snow stuck in his hair. By the time he surfaced, I was out of the tub, and had my loose, long sweater over my head. I was already sticking my arms into my coat.

"You are going to pay for that." He rose up out of that hot tub like an artist's vision of a Greek god, steam curling away from that fine, fine body of his.

"Winner," I said, pointing at my chest while I stomped my wet, cold feet into my dry, cold boots. "Loser." I double-gunned my fingers at him then I made a dash for the stairs.

"Oh, run as far as you like." Ryder's voice was as low and dark as winter honey. "No one's gonna hear you scream way out here. Plus, I know where you're sleeping tonight."

"Who said anything about sleeping?" I was at the sliding glass door, my hand on the handle.

He hadn't even put on his shirt yet, so I wisely spent a portion of my escape time ogling his muscles. My heart thrummed and every nerve in my body zinged with joy, and need, and, okay, a glass of wine.

"You think that's how it's gonna go?" he asked. "I'm just going to forgive your betrayal and let you ravage my body?"

"Nothing you can do about it," I said. "Winners make the rules."

A scream broke through the night, freezing us both in place. The adrenalin pumping through my veins switched to *danger, save, protect*.

"Shit," I tugged the door open and ran into the house, searching for my gun.

Ryder was on my heels, his shirt only over one arm so far, his boots in his hands.

"Cell reception?" I took the time to kick off my boots and get into pants. I couldn't help anyone if I went out there with my pants off and froze to death.

"Out on the main road." He was in his pants, shoving his feet in boots, but still hadn't gotten his other arm in the shirt. "And no, I'm not calling in the cavalry while you go out into a dark forest on your own."

"I can take care—"

"I know. The answer's still no." He tossed a hat and gloves my way. "We do this together. Got that, Mrs. Hyphen Reed?"

I wanted to be annoyed, but he was doing the right thing, making the right choice. In extreme conditions like this, bad weather, terrible visibility, out in the middle of nowhere, it was stupid to split up before we knew what we were dealing with.

"Fine."

A second scream called out, this one lower, more guttural.

We scrambled into our gear, grabbed the emergency flashlights hanging near the sliding door, and pushed into the night with speed.

My head had been a little floaty from the wine but was now brutally clear as I jogged down the deck steps and onto the new fallen snow, flashlight turning the white into diamonds, crystals, glitter.

I took three steps and immediately sank up to my knees. "Sonofabitch," I growled. "It came from over there, right?"

"I think so. The clearing."

Another scream busted through the stillness. I

171

angled in that direction, lifting my knees almost to my chin for each step, trying to break a path as quickly and quietly as possible and despairing that I could accomplish neither.

"There," Ryder pointed. "I see light."

I followed his hand and made for the line of trees to our right.

My breathing was loud in my ears, my heart hammering so hard, I could feel it in my throat.

Another scream called out, then another, and I broke into an awkward run, the only thought in my head to protect, to save, to help whoever was out here, in the middle of nowhere, screaming in the night where no living being could hear them.

The trees lined the edge of a hill and peppered down the slope. I was willing to throw myself down that hill, skate, sled, slip and slide to the bottom and deal with whatever danger I found there.

But Ryder's big hand grabbed at my arm, missed, and hooked the edge of my coat instead.

"We have to—" I said.

He pulled me toward him, only letting go when both our shoulders were against a tree trunk, angled so that we could see the glade below.

"Look," he said.

It took me a second, all my senses hopped up and running through disaster scenarios. Kidnapping, murder, torture, all equal possibilities in my mind.

And behind all those thoughts: *Don't let Ryder get hurt. Don't let him be taken away from me yet. Please, not yet.*

But the sight that greeted me was not a murder scene. Or at least not like any I'd ever seen before.

The clearing was filled with lights, and all of those lights were moving.

My brain simply couldn't make any sense of what was happening.

"What… is that?" I gasped, swallowing hard because gulping down that much frozen air during our run had done a job on my throat and lungs. "What's going on with those people?"

Ryder was breathing hard next to me. I heard the dry click of his throat before he said. "I don't think they're people."

"What do you…?" Then my brain snapped it together.

The clearing was a circular grove. A wide stream cracked through it, water reflecting the lights moving along both banks, lights which were attached to people.

Or, yeah, maybe not humans, but human-like creatures.

One of them warbled, another screeched like an owl, and then there was a song, made of growls and grunts and whistles and hums, a wild, deep, fluid thing that turned the sounds of nature into a symphony.

Like no song I'd ever heard before.

"Bigfoots," Ryder breathed. "Is this… Flip was going to a reunion, right?"

I nodded.

"Is this it? The Bigfoots' family reunion, or gathering of the clans, or…?"

"I don't know," I said. "I've never asked him where it

was exactly. I didn't think he'd want to say. They're very private, the 'Foots."

"So we should go back to the cabin?" Ryder hadn't moved. He loved being an eyewitness to all the supernaturals in Ordinary who made up the stories and myths he'd been reading since he was a kid.

From the tone of his voice, he really, really wanted to watch the Bigfoots at least a moment more before we left them to their privacy.

"Yes. But not yet."

He threw me a glance.

"We need to make sure that screaming was celebratory and no one is hurt." I turned off my flashlight because it wasn't doing any good, and I didn't want to distract the creatures below.

Ryder switched his off too.

"Right," he said, nodding quickly. "Right. Come here." He tugged on me. I didn't fight it. I liked him pulling me to him, as if he had to have more contact, as if his heart was still racing with some of the fear I'd felt.

I was soon smooshed up against him, my back to his front, his arms locked tightly around me as we leaned shoulders into the tree.

The celebration below seemed to be just getting started. As we counted the moments with our breaths, our heartbeats aligning to the rhythm of this ancient song, we saw more Bigfoots enter the glade from the opposite side of the grove.

"Ten bucks that stuff is stolen," Ryder said, and I had to muffle a laugh, because, yeah, I thought it might be.

These Bigfoots were each lit up in various manners. One seemed to have tied hundreds of glow sticks into its hair, so its entire body was dripping with a curtain of glowing orange, pink, and green. Another was covered in round, battery-operated touch lights that it was touching and tapping to the rhythm of the beat.

Another wore what I could only assume was a miner's helmet with band upon band of lights strapped on the helmet, on wrists, arms, and on a very clever crisscross harness that wobbled and shook as the Bigfoots walked.

No, not walked.

"They're dancing," Ryder said.

I nodded, tucking my face down deeper into the neck of my coat. They were indeed dancing. And from the sway and bobbing of the Bigfoots near the stream, it looked like they were enjoying the show.

A whistle, off key and loud, cut through the music. A hush fell over the glade.

Then one voice sang out, deep and warbling like a *dung chen*, the Tibetan horn, melancholy, yet powerful.

The hush turned into a murmur. It looked like everyone down there was excited by this turn of events.

At the northwest edge of the clearing, came a Bigfoot. This one was resplendent in light bulbs, all of them glowing and flickering in a wide, high-collared cape that swooshed and flowed as he strode into the glade like a knight returned.

I knew this Bigfoot was a he for three reasons: one: the light bulb cape; two: the traffic light winking red, yellow, green that he wore on his chest like plate armor;

and three: the fricking light post he stabbed into the ground with each step like a lighted scepter.

"Holy shit," Ryder murmured. "It's Flip."

It was indeed Flip, and I was getting a big ol' eye full of Ordinary's stolen property.

"He told me he didn't steal that stuff," I said.

"Well, good thing your finely honed bullshit meter caught right on to him."

I tried to elbow the man, but he just chuckled and held me tighter.

The murmur in the glade tapered off, and the music began again, changing rhythm so the dancers, Flip now among them, could make their way like electric models strutting a catwalk toward the audience.

Once they reached the edge of the stream, they stopped and stood very still, winking and blinking in the glittery snow-diamond field.

The music halted. The world was silent in the muffled darkness for one, two, three, and then a hum, soft and sweet, drifted up and up. The melody echoed; the harmonies shifted in layers.

At the peak of the octave, the song went back to hums and growls and grunts, a vocal rhythm section. One of the watchers on the bank of the stream stepped forward, wove between the electric 'Foots, and stopped in front of Glow Stick.

There was a very human "*awww…*" and a soft clapping as the couple wandered off, hand in hand toward the woods.

Another figure by the stream stepped away from the

rest. This time Miner Helmet was chosen to stroll into the woods among gentle applause.

A third watcher sashayed away from the river and hopped into the arms of Round Lights, who hooted a little victory warble. There was chuckling, then applause as they trundled into the trees.

"Are we watching the Bigfoot Bachelor?" Ryder asked. "Because it really looks like Bigfoot Bachelor."

"Why isn't anyone picking Flip?" I asked. "He said his heart was here, right? Where are they?"

We weren't the only ones who seemed worried about this. At first, I thought the song was starting up again. But the murmur and voices that rose were not a song. They were questions and whispers and little sounds of concern.

"Eeee-oooo!" a voice called out so loud, I jumped.

"You okay there, Chief?" Ryder chuckled.

"That sounded close."

He nodded. "Look to our left. Careful."

I slowly turned my head.

If not for the small, lit-up heart necklace they wore, I wouldn't have even seen the Bigfoot pushing silently— and I mean absolutely silently—through the snow and trees about twenty feet away.

Heart was moving fast. The absence of light made it hard to tell, but I'd say this Bigfoot was lighter haired than Flip and maybe just a little shorter.

The murmur from below shifted. This time it was a song again, the rhythm matching Heart's supernaturally speedy approach.

Flip stood taller, posed like a king, lamppost scepter

straight in front of him, traffic light refinements flickering red, yellow, green, and cape of light bulbs shifting with little glass-bulb clatters.

I had no idea how he was powering that getup, but obviously Bigfoots knew their way around a light bulb.

Then Heart was there, on the opposite side of the stream. The music changed, switching to just the rhythm again, just a beat. But Heart didn't wait for the song to become more. Heart hopped across the stones in the stream and was on the other side almost instantly.

Flip held still. So very still.

"Come on," Ryder whispered. "You got this."

I was holding my breath.

Then Heart pressed a palm to the lamp post, walked around Flip, one finger trailing over glass and filament, and stopped in front of him again.

Heart's palm rested against the traffic light, right over Flip's heart.

Flip made a very small questioning sound. Heart answered in a sweet warble, touched Flip's cheek, then scooped up Flip's free hand.

The Bigfoots clapped, louder this time. There was laughter and relief in the voices as they left the clearing, walking arm in arm to disappear into the trees.

I exhaled. "Aw, he got his Heart. Lucky guy."

Ryder's arms tightened around me. "Yeah. I know how he feels."

"Ryder Bailey, are you going romantic on me?"

"Maybe."

"I approve. Let's go back to the cabin."

"But they're still doing stuff down there." He

sounded like a little kid who wanted an extra scoop of ice cream. "Bigfoot stuff."

They were still doing Bigfoot stuff. As a matter of fact, it looked like the reunion was just getting started. There was a lot of hooting and hollering. It was loud and was probably only going to get louder.

"Well, you go ahead and stay here. I'm going back to the cabin, the fireplace, and the wine. Also, I plan to be naked."

Ryder let go of me so quickly, I laughed. "Get moving, Mrs. Hyphen." He held his hand out for me, and I took it. "We've got a vacation to get to."

The Bigfoots shouted and howled. Loud. They were really loud.

Something moved in the brush near the house, and a steaming Bigfoot dashed away through the trees.

"Was that guy in our hot tub?" Ryder clicked on his flashlight and sent the beam after the disappearing interloper. "He was in our hot tub!"

I laughed.

The chorus of voices only increased as we trudged uphill through the snow.

Another Bigfoot appeared several yards to our left, rolling a huge boulder. He gave it a push, sending it down the hill. But his aim was off. It smashed into a tree, cracking the trunk and sending great globs of snow to *thunk* to the ground.

"Just the two of us," Ryder said, as the Bigfoot made a sound like swearing, then pushed the boulder to one side to send it rolling down the hill again.

The Bigfoot held still, watching. We held still, watching.

Finally a huge splash sounded as the boulder plowed into the stream. A cheer rose up from the glade below.

There was another rumble, another splash, and more cheering.

"Is this a thing?" Ryder asked. "Boulder bowling?"

"In bowling you try to hit the pins. I think they're trying to miss them."

A solid crack of rock hitting tree broke through the rest of the growing noise.

"So much solitude," I said, following our previous footsteps back to the cabin.

We made it to the door, and yep, there were huge footprints left on the deck by the hot tub, but it seemed like most of the commotion was out in the trees and down in the glade.

I opened the door, and Ryder followed me into the warm, cozy space.

Even though the Bigfoots were making a hullabaloo below us, even though we'd need to lock the door and secure the hot tub and maybe the truck, even though this middle of nowhere somehow meant we weren't alone, or really, monster free, it was amazing.

This was amazing.

"If I'd known they were meeting here," Ryder peeled off gloves and coat, and secured his firearm and flashlight, "I would have picked one of the other half-a-dozen cabins I was looking at."

He threw little glances my way, worried, as I stripped off my outer gear.

"So, um…" he started. "I don't think we can get back over the pass. But I can drive out and find cell reception and maybe see if another—"

I took the few steps that separated us and kissed him.

His response was instant and hot, his hands clutching at the long sweater I still wore, tugging it away from my back slightly, then smoothing it against my back, my hip.

I took extra time with his lips, not trying to bruise, but not being overly careful. He pressed for me to open my mouth, which I did, letting him in willingly.

The kiss went from hot and passionate, to soft and drugging, to slow and languid as we pulled apart and drew back together again, once, twice, three times.

When I finally pulled away, his eyes were glassy and unfocused, his lips swollen, his cheeks and neck flushed. "Um… What?" he said, blinking slowly.

"Solitude," I said, walking backward. I caught his hand.

"Just the two of us." He wove our fingers together, moving with me now.

"Heaven." I guided us back and back, past the heat of the fireplace, through the warm glowing hall, and finally, *finally*, to the private, cozy bedroom.

"Let the perfect vacation begin," I said.

Ryder gave me a wicked smile and locked the door behind him.

AT DEATH'S DOOR

AN ORDINARY MAGIC STORY

THAN NEVER DREADED opening doors. He was, after all, the god of death. There was nothing behind any door that could cause him lasting concern. However, he had just brewed the potentially perfect cup of hot cocoa and had yet to taste it.

Therefore, the knock upon his door was inconvenient and opening said door, a terrible annoyance.

The door handle was smooth and cool in his palm, cooler than he would have expected before he had lain his powers down to vacation as a mortal. But then, his days spent in the town for vacationing gods had been peppered with numerous surprises.

Even some delights.

The knocked paused. He knew who was on the other side of the door: a woman who owed him a favor.

Excellent.

He turned the handle and pulled.

Delaney Reed was smiling. She did that a lot around him. If pressed, he might admit he enjoyed that aspect of the woman who allowed and disallowed gods to vacation in this town.

However, if pressed by Delaney Reed on the subject he would undoubtedly find a way to avoid answering her.

It was more entertaining that way.

"Reed Daughter," he said.

"Just Delaney," she corrected for the six-hundred and forty-fourth time.

Yes, he had been counting.

"So, are you still on for this?" she asked.

The weather was barbarically rough, wind and rain determined to commit destruction and flood. The radio stations, television, and other broadcast services were warning that this winter storm could generate hurricane force. Knock out electrical power. Tear down trees.

Tomorrow, Than would be required to assist with clean up. He was looking forward to it. Being a part of constructive change, instead of his rather natural state of chaotic change, pleased him.

"The pet-sitting? Remember?" Delaney lifted a bright orange leash that was attached to the very good boy, Spud, who was Ryder and Delaney's dog of questionable breeding. Certainly border collie and chow chow were involved.

Spud sat, face tipped up and tongue hanging out, being the well-trained dog he was.

Next to him was a less desirable creature.

The dragon.

Than sniffed in disapproval.

The dragon had taken a moderately clever disguise.

No one would expect a little pink piglet to actually be a massive, powerful, fire-breathing dragon.

Mortals and most supernaturals saw only the outside of a thing. The dragon's outside was, according to several sources, adorable.

Than did not hold the same opinion.

The dragon tipped its head up, eyes burning red, smoke curling from its nostrils and ears.

It growled.

"Unless you've changed your mind?" Delaney asked.

Than narrowed his eyes at the dragon and considered growling back.

"I have not." He held his hand out for the leash. "You will owe me a favor, as we agreed."

"Worth it," she said with a fast grin. "Let me get their food and other stuff. It will only take a sec." She jogged off into the rain and wind toward her vehicle. In a hurry, as most mortals were.

"Spud," Than greeted the dog. The dog wagged its tail but remained sitting. "Come into my home." Than stepped to the side so the dog could pass.

The dog hopped up and trotted into the house, nails clicking softly on the hardwood floor.

The dragon remained.

Than stared at the dragon. The dragon stared back.

Delaney jogged up to the porch. Something bright bounced away from the stack of things she carried, but she didn't appear to notice.

"Spud gets two scoops, one in the morning, one at night. He likes a little wet food with it, and treats are in the bag. I packed his favorite toys and some chew bones and his bed. He'll try to get up on your bed with you. If you let him sleep with you, be ready to get your ears licked at four o'clock in the morning.

"Dragon pig only needs to eat once a day, but it needs to be something big. Little snacks won't hold it over. I made a list of sheds and fences and old vehicles we've gotten the okay for it to eat. If you don't want to take it all over town for meals, you can just go to the junkyard. We have an account with them. No more than one car-sized item a day."

The dragon grunted, apparently displeased with that rule.

"I shall be diligent in my application of your requests."

The dragon growled, and the wet air filled with the smell of campfire.

Than ignored it.

Delaney hustled into the house without asking, he supposed because she had been there twice before. Than remained by the open door. The dragon remained on the front step. Both watched as the Bridge of god power —the only being who could allow a god to vacation in this clever little beach town called Ordinary—settled items for the dog and dragon onto Than's dining table.

"Okay, that's it. Oh, and Spud's favorite thing is fetching the tennis ball for dragon pig to push around with its nose." She put hands on her hips and chewed her lower lip. "I think that's all. I'll want a full report. Especially on dragon pig. Don't let it act like a dragon out in public. No flames. No flying. Okay?"

"Reed Daughter," he said.

"Delaney."

Six-hundred and forty-five.

"Is there some other reason you remain here?" Than asked.

"No," she said, the word carried by a strong breath. "No, this is great. Really great of you to help." She bent and gave Spud a scratch, a pet, and cupped his face between her palms. "You be a really good boy, Spuddo. We'll be back soon."

Spud wagged his tail and tried to lick her fingers. She scrubbed behind his ears one more time, then turned.

"Are you going to let dragon pig into your house?"

Than considered the value of truth and lies and leaving the beast out in the rain. It was a dragon. It had no actual need to spend time inside a small timber structure. It was far sturdier than timber or siding or roofing ever could be.

"Than?" she asked.

The dragon pig squealed with convincing baby pig distress.

"It usually stays inside," she said, her gaze taking in Than's expression. "Spud really likes it inside with him. They're buddies. They do best if they're together most of the time."

Spud heard his name and walked over to Than, stopping to lean against his leg while sniffing at his shoe. His tail swished and swished.

"I see," Than said, then to the dragon, "You may enter my home."

The dragon grunted in satisfaction and trotted into

the house like it owned the place. Spud yipped once and galloped happily after it.

Than's gaze tracked the dragon's progress while it investigated the room, the furniture, and each of Than's precious potted plants.

It stopped in front of the fiddle leaf tree fig, opened its mouth, and leaned toward the plant.

Than snapped his fingers once. Not using power. No, that wasn't allowed here, but the threat was clear.

The dragon wisely jerked back, jaws shutting with a boulder-breaking crack. Clouds puffed from its nostrils. It growled and moved away from the plants toward the hallway.

"Remember, full report," Delaney said. "No dragon fire stuff. Do you think you've got this? I could go over the food thing again…"

Delaney had that tone in her voice. The one he didn't like. It was thick and upward drifting. Strained. He believed it was worry.

The dragon was halfway down the hall now, trotting with purpose.

"I mean, you'll have to remember to let Spud out in the yard to do his business, but dragon pig doesn't really do that stuff. It likes to go out with Spud though, so you can just let them…"

The dragon chugged forward like an industrial age locomotive engine, smoke trailing the air behind it.

It was chugging toward Than's bedroom.

His *private* bedroom.

"There is no need," he said, ushering Delaney to

exit by way of the open door. "Enjoy your time away. I shall collect the favor in due time."

"Are you sure you don't need—"

Than slammed the door in her face.

The dragon was nowhere to be seen.

Spud, however, stood in the hall, tail wagging uncertainly as he stared into the darkness.

"You are a pleasant companion. Loyal and refreshingly simplistic in your needs." Than snapped his fingers again. Spud spun a quick circle and romped to Than's side, panting and wriggling for all his worth.

Than allowed his fingers to dangle and Spud positioned his head under them, his face going blissful when Than scratched behind his ears.

"I do not know why you associate with that creature. It is nothing like you." Than hadn't been speaking overly loud. The storm outside rattled against the roofing, the gutters, and the windows.

But the dragon in the other room growled. It was annoyed.

Excellent.

"It has been years since I've slain a dragon," Than mused.

The dragon growled again. Louder.

Spud wasn't listening. The dog was now interested in the front door. He sniffed it, whined at it, scratched it with a single swipe of his paw, then whined again.

Than wasn't speaking to the dog, in any case. Threatening the dragon seemed a sporting way to remind it that he was Death. *The* Death.

An invasion of his bedroom would not be tolerated.

"I am suddenly of mind to take up my power and leave my vacation behind."

Spud bumped his nose into Than's knee and whined at the door again.

Ah, yes. Delaney had mentioned outdoors for the dog to do business. Than opened the door, waited for Spud to bark and rush out into the rain, then closed the door again.

Time to deal with the dragon.

"I have given the eldest Reed a promise," Than said. "I will follow the rules she set for your supervision. Therefore, you will follow my orders."

Spud's barking had changed, sounding more vigorous.

The bedroom door clicked open and, after a second, slammed. Pig hooves approached.

Than fought the urge to smile. This was going better than he'd expected.

The dragon came into the light. It was still in that ridiculous pig disguise. Soft and round and pink.

Only now it had a large, fuzzy, spider slipper clenched in its overly sharp dragon teeth.

"No," Than said.

The dragon growled, smoke curling around its head.

"Put my slipper down."

The dragon's eyes kindled hot.

"Do not eat——"

The spider slipper flashed into a ball of flames: fur, eyes, and eight wobbly legs disintegrating into a cloud of ash in an instant.

"——my slipper."

The dragon belched ash.

Than glared, one long finger pointed. "You," he commanded. "Outside with the dog. I order it so."

He pulled the door open with such speed it sucked rain over the threshold.

The dragon glowered at Death, then glared at the rainy weather. It grunted in surprise and ran to the door.

"That is much better." But Than was looking out the door now too.

What he had not known, and had not been concerned about, was the unlatched gate, open toward the road, swinging in the wind.

What he was now concerned about was Spud, who had discovered the open gate some time ago, as the dog was already two streets down and running north, fast.

The dragon growled.

"This is not ideal," Than said.

The dragon grunted in agreement.

"I am less confident in assuming the behavior of dogs, but I believe it will not return here on instinct alone."

The dragon rumbled. It almost sounded like *idiot*.

"Right then." Than pulled on his long coat, rubber galoshes, and brimmed hat. "We shall find him and bring him back. Since you are to appear to be a pet, I shall treat you as one."

He plucked the bright orange leash off of the table, letting it hang to untangle.

The dragon trotted up and set it on fire.

Than sighed and threw the fiery leash out into the rain. The flames snuffed out in a wink.

"I am not impressed," Than said. "You will obey my every word."

The dragon snarled.

"As Delaney would expect of you. Your ability to behave like a pig will feature highly in the report I will be submitting."

The dragon grunted.

Then it *oink*ed like a good little piggy and fell into step at Than's side.

They left the house.

And if the smell of campfire and smoke mixed with the wind and rain, well, no one was out in the weather to report it.

———

"BY ALL MEANS," THAN said. "That toilet is dreadful."

The dragon unhinged its jaw and swallowed the commode in one bite.

Than supposed Mr. Tarr would file a complaint about stolen yard art. That would create extra paperwork at the station and a search for something that was not stolen, but instead, eaten.

As Delaney would say: Worth it.

The dragon grumbled, and they continued down the neighborhood street. Spud was just in sight, three blocks up. Than had called for him multiple times, but the dog had not glanced back once.

The dragon grunted at a rusted anchor. It wasn't

even attached to a boat but was rather uselessly leaning against a tree.

"Be quick."

The anchor went down in a shot.

At the next block, the dragon grunted at a statue of a fish with far too many teeth, protruding eyes, and garish colors.

"I would feed that to you by the spoonful," Than said.

The dragon crunched it down in three bites.

Several blocks north, Than paused to debate the pros and cons of insisting the dragon eat a pop-up travel trailer. The trailer was covered in moss and sludge, with only a broken bumper and a Keep On Trucking sticker visible.

Pro: It would rid the neighborhood of that bumper sticker.

Con: It would unhouse several raccoons and a skunk.

Before he had made up his mind, a squeal of locked brakes, a thunderous crash, and one small, sharp yelp cut through the rain.

Than held very still. Even though his powers were at rest here in Ordinary, he was Death. If someone—if Spud—were dead, he would know.

He opened his senses to his more godly vision, looking for Spud's light, his spirit.

An arc of green light rose out and up, the life spirit of an old tree turning the clouds emerald for a moment. Smaller green sparks from dying plant life fizzed upward in a steady sparkling stream around him, mixing with the white of the driving rain.

Life sparks of birds, mice, grasshoppers, and other small creatures winged to the sky, while more liquid orbs of fish, crabs, and sea lions tumbled across the land before swooping back westward to the raging waves.

There were deaths, many deaths, but there was no wandering Spud spirit.

He was not dead, but he could be hurt.

Than and the dragon broke into a sprint, both covering more ground than either should be able to if they were simply human and pig.

The next street was Highway 101, the main north-south thoroughfare.

Than was expecting a traffic accident.

Than was expecting to find Spud panting, thrown hard to the asphalt, broken.

Than was not expecting to find a rather large old tree had fallen across a portion of the road.

More than one car had skidded to a stop, but some-how, they had avoided hitting or being hit by the downed tree.

To Than's great relief they had also avoided hitting Spud.

Than hurried to the crosswalk, his long-legged pace carrying him as quickly as a human ought to move. He splashed across the intersection, one hand tight on his hat, coat whipping, and rain soaking through his trouser legs.

The dragon led Than by a slight margin.

Than stopped on one side of the tree, peering

through the huge branches to the golden dog within them.

Spud was unharmed, not a single branch having touched him.

He was, however, trapped.

Than considered the many ways he could free the dog. All of them involved magic, god power, or heavy equipment.

Spud whined, pushed against a branch, and wagged his tail hopefully.

The dragon grumbled. Grunted twice.

Than looked down.

The dragon tipped its head. A tiny flame shot out of its mouth.

"Delaney expressly forbade you to do anything to reveal your true nature."

The dragon grumbled. Than understood the language of dragons enough to know what *stupid* sounded like.

"She will ask."

The dragon growled.

"She will insist on a full report. I will tell her the full truth."

The dragon looked at Spud, glanced at Than, and then, having made a decision, worked through the branches. It burned them off with laser-thin flames, the rain dousing the fire before it spread.

When the dragon reached Spud, the dog wiggled and whined, rubbing alongside his buddy.

The dragon huffed, touched its nose very gently to

Spud's, then *oink*ed and led him out of the tangle until both were at Than's feet.

"Spud," Than said. "Why have you caused such concern? You will come with me now."

Spud spit out a ball. A bright ball the exact color of the object Delaney had accidentally dropped.

"Is this it then? The root of our trouble?" Than picked up the wet, gritty ball and pocketed it.

No one had been harmed. The cars could easily avoid the few branches that blocked part of the road. Several people were on their phones, undoubtedly calling for someone to take care of the fallen tree.

That someone would probably be Myra Reed, Delaney's sister who also served with her on the force.

Since Than was only a Reserve Officer and did not remember tree removal listed in his job duties, he turned away from the foliage.

"We will return to my house in an orderly fashion," he declared. "March."

The dragon and dog did as he said, and the walk back was quicker, though no drier.

Once inside, Than mopped Spud with his softest towel, fed him exactly one scoop of food with wet on top, and filled the other bowl with water.

Spud ate it all, tail wagging.

Good.

Than poured his forsaken cocoa down the sink and began brewing a new cup.

When he sat with what might be the perfect cup of cocoa, Spud walked over and curled up at his feet.

The dragon, who had spent all of the time since

their return stacking Spud's toys into a pile, abandoned the task for no reason Than could discern. It trotted along the edge of the room, ignoring the plants and ignoring Than.

That was also good.

Than lifted his cup from the saucer and blew across the top to cool it. Before he could press his lips to the rim, his phone rang.

He glanced at the screen and sighed.

"Yes, Myra Reed?" he answered.

Delaney's sister sounded like she was in the middle of the road directing traffic. "Do you know anything about the tree that fell on 101?"

"What might I know?"

"Why some of the branches are burned through."

The dragon threw a glance at Than. It looked a little panicked before it turned its attention to its hooves as if they were the most fascinating thing in the universe.

"Branches burned through?" Than repeated. "How odd."

"Does that mean you know about it? People saw you there."

The dragon looked up. Narrowed its eyes.

"I know nothing about a fallen tree or burned limbs," Than said, holding the dragon's gaze.

The dragon's eyes went wide. Its jaw dropped open, tongue falling out with a thin puff of steam.

"Uh-huh," Myra said. "Is that what you'd tell Delaney if she were the one calling you?"

"It is. Now, if that is all, I have other matters to attend."

"Anything I should know about? Curses? Dead bodies? Your new girlfriend?"

"Good-bye, Myra Reed."

Than placed the phone on the side table.

Spud propped his head on Than's stockinged foot. After a moment, the dragon shuffled over, grunted at Than once, then snuggled up against the dog. The dragon's warm, hearth-fire breath drifted across Than's ankles.

The storm outside raged cold and fierce, the dog and dragon snored, and Than finally lifted the cup and took a sip. He closed his eyes and savored the bitter and the sweet of cocoa, sugar, and cream.

It might not be perfect. But it was not terrible at all.

ACKNOWLEDGMENTS

I'd like to thank the talented people who have helped me bring this installment of Ordinary Magic to life.

Thank you to Lou Harper of Cover Affairs for yet another amazing Ordinary cover. You're right. Tentacles are fun!

My heartfelt gratitude to my copy editor Sharon Elaine Thompson, for your sharp eyes and snappy grammar fixes. Thank you oodles to my amazing beta reader, Dejsha Knight, for always being willing to read on short notice.

I'd also like to give an extra shout-out of gratitude to my fine fellow writers who graciously shared the Dirty Deeds collection with me, without which, this book would not have been written. RJ Blaine, Faith Hunter, and Diana Pharaoh Francis, thank you for the companionship, laughter, and wild ride!

To my husband, Russ, and my sons, Kameron and Konner, I love you, always. You are the best part of my life. Thank you for sharing your lives with me.

And finally, to you, dear readers: Thank you for spending a little time at Oregon's most magical vacation destinations. I hope you come back soon!

ABOUT THE AUTHOR

DEVON MONK is a USA Today bestselling fantasy author. Her series include Ordinary Magic, Souls of the Road, West Hell Magic, House Immortal, Allie Beckstrom, Broken Magic and the Age of Steam steampunk series. She also writes all sorts of short stories which can be found in various anthologies and in her collection: A Cup of Normal.

She lives happily beneath the lovely, rainy skies of Oregon. When not writing, Devon can be found drinking too much coffee, watching hockey, and knitting silly things.

Want to read more from Devon?

Follow her blog, sign up for her newsletter, or check out the links below.

ALSO BY DEVON MONK

House Immortal

Infinity Bell

Crucible Zero

BROKEN MAGIC

Hell Bent

Stone Cold

Backlash

ALLIE BECKSTROM

Magic to the Bone

Magic in the Blood

Magic in the Shadows

Magic on the Storm

Magic at the Gate

Magic on the Hunt

Magic on the Line

Magic without Mercy

Magic for a Price

AGE OF STEAM

Dead Iron

Tin Swift

Cold Copper

Hang Fire (short story)

SHORT STORIES

A Cup of Normal (collection)

Yarrow, Sturdy and Bright (Once Upon a Curse anthology)

A Small Magic (Once Upon a Kiss anthology)

Little Flame (Once Upon a Ghost anthology)

Wish Upon a Straw (Once Upon a Wish anthology)

Printed in Great Britain
by Amazon

25489136R00121